PANDA IN THE PARK

'We have to find that trap,' Mandy said grimly. Her limbs were tired after the exertion of climbing the steps, but she knew that the important thing was to find the deer trap and then at least they would have a clue as to where the mother panda might be.

After a while, she heard James stumble. 'Ouch!' he cried, as a broken pine branch gouged a gash in his cheek. Mandy and Tai An rushed over to help him up. 'I'm OK,' he insisted, as Mandy tried to stop the bleeding with a tissue.

'Let's carry on then,' she said, pulling James to his feet.

'Wait!' James's face was like a ghost's as he pointed to a twisted and rusted bit of metal that was barely visible under a branch of bamboo that was heavily laden with snow. 'That's it, isn't it?' James said, tremulously.

'Yes,' Tai An confirmed sadly. 'I'm afraid it is.'

Mandy gulped as she saw the dark stain in the earth below the trap, along with a clump of white panda fur.

Animal Ark series

LUCY DANIELS

Panda

— *in the* —

Park

Illustrations by Ann Baum

Hodder
Children's
Books

a division of Hodder Headline plc

Special thanks to Kirsty White
Thanks also C. J. Hall, B.Vet.Med., M.R.C.V.S., for reviewing the
veterinary information contained in this book.

Text copyright © 1999 Ben M. Baglio
Created by Ben M. Baglio, London W12 7QY
Illustrations copyright © 1999 Ann Baum

First published in Great Britain in 1999
by Hodder Children's Books

A Catalogue record for this book is available from the British Library

ISBN 0 340 72403 X

Typeset by Avon Dataset Ltd, Bidford-on-Avon, Warks

Printed and bound in Great Britain by
Clays Ltd, St Ives plc

Hodder Children's Books
a division of Hodder Headline plc
338 Euston Road
London NW1 3BH

One

'It's beautiful, but it doesn't feel like China.' Mandy yawned sleepily, as she looked out of the window of the Jeep at the misted landscape. The road was climbing steadily into the mountains of the Sichuan province in southwestern China.

In the soft light of the afternoon, the mountains were a darker shade of blue than the winter sky. The rice fields they'd passed on their journey were frost-tinged dark brown earth. There was no sign of the lush green fields and bamboo forests that Mandy had gazed at in the tourist guides.

'Well, it's not Welford,' James Hunter, Mandy's friend, joked.

Mandy yawned again. 'It's certainly not!' she said, as she had another look round. Despite the familiar mist and the dull winter sky, there were differences – the colours were stronger and the mountains much higher than the hilly moors of Yorkshire. Her heart raced as she saw a large bird lift off from an icy expanse of water and head swiftly towards the fading sun. It was nothing like any of the birds she watched every winter's day in Welford.

Mandy and James, along with Mandy's father, Adam Hope, had arrived in China earlier that day.

Mandy's mother, Emily, had already spent nearly two months in China where she was working with giant pandas. It was a temporary post with an international wildlife charity. Mandy's mum had always been fascinated by these large and lovable animals and, when the opportunity arose, Adam Hope had insisted she accept the job. Locum vet Alastair King had been helping out at Animal Ark, the Hopes' veterinary practice back in Welford, and had taken over while Adam was here in China.

Mandy and James couldn't wait to see a giant panda. As soon as they'd found out that they were going to visit Emily, they had been getting books on pandas from the library and searching the Internet on James's computer for information that would be useful during their trip.

And now they were on the last leg of their journey to the research station in the Qionglai Mountains where Emily was working with a Chinese zoologist, Dr Yun. Dr Yun was famous for her work with giant pandas in the wild and Emily's veterinary expertise would help the zoologist's plan to move the wild pandas on the mountain to the safety of the panda reservation at Wolong.

Adam Hope was sitting in the front seat beside Mr Chang, one of the research station's workers, who had collected the Hopes and James from the airport. Mandy saw her father's tired smile turn into a yawn, reflected in the rear-view mirror of the Jeep.

'You must have jet-lag,' Mr Chang pointed out. 'You've come, what is it, ten thousand kilometres?'

Adam Hope nodded. 'We've been travelling for around thirty-six hours,' he said.

'Ten thousand, three hundred and forty kilometres, to be precise,' James said, 'that's including the distance between Welford and Heathrow airport and the flight from Beijing to here.' He'd worked it out with an atlas and a ruler on the day that his parents, Mr and Mrs Hunter, had agreed that he could go to China with Mandy.

James pushed his glasses up his nose as he yawned too. Mandy smiled at her friend's familiar gesture. 'Is it much further, Mr Chang?' she asked.

'No, we'll soon reach the research station,' Mr Chang replied.

Mandy glanced at her watch. It was later than she thought. She was surprised to realise that she'd slept for almost two hours in the Jeep.

'Might we see pandas on this journey, Mr Chang?' James asked, hopefully.

Mr Chang smiled. 'I don't think so,' he replied. 'Pandas stay away from cars.'

'How many pandas are there on the mountain?' Mandy asked, knowing that few giant pandas remained in the wild.

'Four adult pandas,' Mr Chang told them.

Adam Hope nodded. 'Not enough to survive on their own,' he pointed out.

'That's why we are making a panda corridor,' Mr Chang explained. 'We want to encourage them to travel down the mountain through the corridor, and gather on the reserve, which is rather like a giant wildlife park. They will essentially still be in the wild, but it will be easier for us to monitor and observe them and they will have a better chance of finding a good mate!' He grinned.

'What you need is a Panda Lonely Hearts Club!' James joked. Mandy smiled.

'Have any cubs been born?' she asked Mr Chang.

'Two counted this year. It's been a good year,' he replied.

As they climbed higher up the mountain, the scenery changed. Scattered thickets of bamboo began to appear on the barren slopes. Mandy gazed at the thin stems that sprouted a heavy bush of thick green leaves.

'When I was a boy, all this was bamboo forest.' Mr Chang waved one arm expansively. 'You couldn't see the mountains for bamboo.'

'What happened?' Mandy asked.

Mr Chang shrugged. 'They began to cut it down some years ago. Bamboo was a big export for China at one time.'

'It certainly makes you think twice about using raspberry canes,' Adam Hope remarked, as Mandy thought of her grandfather's lovingly tended cottage garden back in Yorkshire.

'Now the forestry department is making several reservations throughout Sichuan for the pandas,' Mr Chang continued. 'There will be no more bambo-cutting on the reserves. But pandas are greedy. Adults eat fourteen kilograms of bamboo a day!'

'Is there enough bamboo for them here?' Mandy asked anxiously.

'For the four of them and the cubs, yes, but there is not enough for a healthy population,' Mr Chang replied. 'That's why the pandas have to move. There are not enough pandas left to survive in the wild now.'

Mandy blinked. Beside her, James's cheerful expression became distinctly glum.

Mr Chang noticed their silence. 'Not to worry,' he assured them. 'There are many cubs born every year in reservations and at zoos. Soon all the reserves will be linked together by panda corridors.'

'We read about panda corridors on the Internet,' Mandy said, 'but what exactly are they?'

'The proper name is forest habitat links,' Mr Chang explained. 'The plan is to link all the reserves by making wide trails of bamboo, so the pandas can move to the reserves in their own way, eating as they go along.'

'So it's a panda motorway!' James exclaimed.

Mandy laughed. 'Yes, with plenty of motorway cafés.'

Mr Chang nodded. 'That's exactly right.'

Adam Hope turned round to face them. 'If Dr Yun manages to move the pandas on this mountain to the safety of a reservation, they'll be fine,' he added.

'Rick McGinley will help too,' Mr Chang added. 'Rick is from a Canadian wildlife preservation programme. Rick will chase the pandas along the corridor to Wolong – the pandas will go quick, quick, quick!'

Mandy and James laughed at the image of a man chasing pandas along a passage, although they had no idea yet of what Rick looked like.

'The giant panda will survive!' Mr Chang assured them.

As the road climbed higher into the mountains, Mandy and James looked out to see that the bamboo growth was thickening. The engine note changed as Mr Chang turned on to a sharply rising mud track and engaged the four-wheel drive.

'This is some journey,' Adam Hope commented, as the vehicle's wheels struggled to stay on the track that zigzagged up the mountainside.

'It's much easier with the Jeep,' Mr Chang responded. 'Before, I often got stuck. In snow, the track was impassable. Now, no problem.' He grinned broadly as the wheels hit a large boulder and the Jeep lurched. 'Not so much of a problem, anyway,' he said, as he deftly manoeuvred round the obstacle. 'Maybe it was even easier when people used to travel by yak!' He glanced at Mandy and James. 'Before cars came, people used yak to climb the mountain,' he explained. 'The yak is like the mule.'

The Hopes and James laughed nervously as the track became steeper.

'I'll let them know we're here,' Mr Chang said, as he slowed down the Jeep and picked up a radio set, speaking into it in Chinese.

Mandy gazed out expectantly. She hadn't seen her mother for weeks. Although she had enjoyed reading Emily's letters, Mandy was longing to talk to her mother in person and hear all about her time in China.

The bamboo thickets had become a forest now in which bamboo plants grew amongst tall, snow-laden conifers. It was thrilling to know that, somewhere amidst the greenery, giant pandas lived.

Mr Chang's radio message had not been answered. He spoke again, and then waited.

'Is there a problem?' Adam Hope asked him.

Mr Chang shrugged. 'Maybe they don't hear me. It doesn't matter.'

Suddenly, the cloud cover broke and they were in blazing winter sunshine that lit the narrow track like a spotlight. On either side, bamboo grew thickly in leafy fronds that glistened with frost.

Mandy and James looked around in wonder. 'This is amazing,' Mandy exclaimed.

'The giant pandas' home,' James sighed.

Suddenly Mandy caught a glimpse of black and white in the lush growth. She looked again, so excited that she forgot her tiredness. There, peering at her through the bamboo, was a small panda face. A second later it disappeared in a flurry of bamboo leaves. Mandy grabbed James's arm 'Did you see that?' she cried.

James looked thrilled. 'Yes!'

Mandy's heart was beating like a drum. 'There was a panda cub there, Mr Chang!' she said.

Mr Chang stopped the Jeep, frowning thoughtfully. 'What sort of size was it?'

'Not very big,' Mandy replied. 'It only reached halfway up that bamboo bush.'

'That would be about right,' Mr Chang said. 'The cubs are born in August or September, so they're four or five months old now. But it's very strange that one was so far down the mountain. They usually stay above the research station.'

Adam Hope peered into the undergrowth, hoping for a glimpse. 'It's definitely gone,' he said sadly. 'I suppose it ran back to its mother the moment it saw us.

'Don't worry,' Mr Chang consoled them, as he drove off again. 'You'll see more pandas soon.'

As they rounded the next corner they saw a small deer on the track. The deer froze momentarily, then vanished into the undergrowth with an agile leap, leaving only a flutter of brush in its wake as Mandy and James gazed after it.

'Musk deer,' Mr Chang explained. 'The local people trap them for food. In China, we have many poor people. I understand why they have to set the deer traps, but sometimes the pandas can get hurt by accident even though the traps are set far below where the pandas live.' Mr Chang sighed,

then continued, 'When we get the pandas on to the reservation they will be safe from that.' The track had narrowed sharply and he had to concentrate on keeping the wheels within the rutted tracks. When the radio chattered into life, he slowed down again to answer it.

'That was Dr Yun,' he said with a smile, when the call was over. 'She and Mrs Hope are looking forward to seeing you soon at the research station.'

At last, the track levelled into a clearing amidst the pine trees, where they saw a long wooden hut with a roof covered with radio antennae. 'That must be the research station,' James said.

Mandy nodded. Every window was lit and she could see people at work inside. On the other side of the clearing there was a smaller hut, with a rickety-looking tin chimney leaking wispy smoke. Above the wooden door there was a plaque with Chinese writing. Mandy smiled broadly. The thrill of arriving had driven away her fatigue.

As the Jeep stopped, the door of the larger hut opened and Emily Hope walked out with a smiling Chinese woman.

Mandy jumped out of the Jeep and ran over to hug her mother. 'How are you – and how are the pandas?' she asked in a rush.

Emily Hope grinned. She was wrapped up in

warm clothes and a woollen bobble hat hid her red hair. 'Happy New Year to you too!' she teased Mandy, before she hugged Adam Hope and then said hello to James. 'Except it's not New Year in China for a couple of weeks yet; the Chinese celebrate their New Year at the end of January,' she added.

'That's right.' The Chinese lady stepped forward. 'I'm Dr Yun,' she said, shaking hands first of all with Adam and then with Mandy and James.

Mandy was delighted to meet the famous panda expert at last. 'Mum's told me all about your work here,' she said, 'I'm really glad I've got the chance to visit. I know what a great privilege it is.'

'I hope you enjoy your stay,' Dr Yun replied warmly. 'It's a bit late today, but tomorrow I'll show you all round.'

Once they'd thanked Mr Chang for the lift, the Hopes and James followed Dr Yun and Emily into the smaller of the two huts, where Dr Yun showed Mandy and James to their sleeping cubicles at the rear. Hastily, Mandy unpacked her rucksack and put her things away in a rickety cupboard that stood between the two narrow wooden bunks. Each had a surrounding rail and a cotton curtain to pull round to make separate sleeping compartments.

When she and James went to the common room

at the front of the hut, Emily and Adam Hope were talking to Dr Yun and a sturdily built man with a thick red beard. Mandy and James went over to them and each took a seat on one of the hard wooden stools that were arranged around a stove.

'Hello,' the man said, in a deep, gruff, Canadian accent, 'I'm Rick McGinley. I'm the gofer around here.'

Emily smiled. 'Rick's a doctor of zoology. He's worked at San Diego Zoo, so he's something of a panda expert, although he's more experienced with pandas in captivity.'

'Dr Yun's teaching me all about pandas in their natural habitat,' Rick explained. 'Knowing more about the way pandas behave in the wild will help us to protect them in the reservations.'

Mandy nodded as another Chinese lady came through a door with a tray of tea and buns. As she poured fragrant tea into small cups, she said something in Chinese. 'Our cook tells me that dinner will be ready soon!' Dr Yun translated.

Mandy sipped the tea slowly. It was unlike the tea she was used to drinking, but it had a delicate, pleasant taste. The buns were delicious, with sweet crumbly pastry and a filling that tasted a bit like custard. The combination of food and warmth made her sleepy again and she had to struggle to keep her eyes open. As she glanced round the common room, she noticed it was filled with ramshackle furniture that was quite out of keeping with the businesslike air of the place. It was strange to think that people had both lived and worked here for years.

'So what did you learn at Chengdu?' she asked her mum. Emily had spent six weeks working at the zoo where many of the world's captive pandas lived.

'That I have a lot to learn about how to treat pandas!' Emily joked. 'I did do an introductory course on acupuncture, though.'

'So you'll be able to stick a couple of pins into a sick animal and save us all that money we spend on anaesthetics,' Adam Hope teased her.

'No,' Emily confessed, 'but I've learned how to treat arthritis and maybe I'll manage to treat certain skin problems as well. There's a college in England that does courses so I'm hoping to do a course by correspondence when I get back home.' She chuckled. 'I might even manage to do something about your expanding waistline, for that matter!'

Adam Hope looked guilty – he had just finished a second bun.

James looked worried. 'Doesn't it hurt the animals when you stick the pins in?' he asked.

Emily shook her head. 'No more than when you give them a booster inoculation. Acupuncture is very gentle. You leave the pins in for twenty minutes or so and then take them out. You have to keep an eye on the patient to make sure they don't take the pins out for you, though!'

Mr Hope and Mandy laughed. Animal Ark's patients sometimes didn't understand that the vets were trying to help them.

'By the way, did you remember to bring a stock of the antibiotics I mentioned that we'd find useful over here?' Emily asked Adam.

He nodded. 'They're in my case, along with a few other things that I thought might come in useful.'

'That's very good of you,' Dr Yun said. 'Although we can make most drugs in China, we've found that some Western antibiotics are better than ours. But they're expensive and we can't afford to buy all that we need.'

'I'm glad to be able to help,' Adam told her. 'And thank you for the opportunity to come and see your work.'

'With luck, we won't need to use the antibiotics too often,' Emily said, as Mandy tried to stifle a yawn.

Rick nodded. 'We only really need them if one

of the pandas gets hurt in a deer trap or some-thing.'

Mandy and James glanced at each other. 'Can't you stop people trapping deer?' James asked.

Dr Yun smiled sadly. 'The workers check for traps regularly,' she explained. 'But, especially in winter when there's often not enough food to go round, there are too many traps to find, and sometimes the traps are set higher up the mountain than they should be. It's sad, but people have to eat.'

Rick nodded. 'In the winter, the pandas go further down the mountain. We do everything we can to prevent it but there's always a risk.'

The cook came out again and hit a gong on the veranda outside the hut. One by one, the research station's workers appeared, taking off their thick cotton jackets and heavy boots as they entered the hut.

As Mandy listened to the workers chatting away to one another she looked round the room and noticed a display of pictures and maps on the far wall of the common room. 'That explains what we're doing here,' Rick told her, when he saw her interest.

'Let's go and have a look,' James suggested.

Before Mandy and James reached the display they were interrupted as the door of the hut burst open again and a young girl appeared. She didn't bother to take off her jacket but immediately launched into a flood of rapid Chinese. Mandy and James paused as Dr Yun jumped up and began to question the girl.

Rick listened, frowning.

'What's happening?' Mandy asked him anxiously.

'I'm not sure,' he muttered, 'I didn't catch all of it.'

Dr Yun turned to Emily and Adam. 'A panda is sick!' she announced. 'We need your help.'

'What's wrong?' Emily Hope asked, frowning.

'It's Li Li, our oldest female,' Dr Yun replied. 'The worker who found her says she's been hurt by a deer trap!'

Mandy's heart began to thud wildly as Emily Hope told Adam to fetch the drugs he had brought from Yorkshire. 'What can we do?' she asked.

Emily smiled thinly. 'You'll have to wait here. It's best if there are as few of us as possible. Pandas are wary of humans by nature, especially if they are sick, and we mustn't risk making her any worse.'

Two

Mandy gazed forlornly at the steaming food on the table. Although the stir-fried vegetables were delicious, she was too worried about the injured panda to enjoy her food. Mandy preferred not to eat meat and she had been glad that there were bowls of sticky rice and assorted vegetables as well as a dish of chicken and another of crispy wind-dried beef, but she had only been able to eat a little.

'That was good!' James exclaimed, when he had finished his meal. As always, his healthy appetite was not affected by what was happening. When Mandy didn't reply, he stared at her. 'You're thinking about the panda, aren't you?'

Mandy nodded. She had been watching the hand move round on her watch. Half an hour had passed since her parents had left with Dr Yun and Rick. 'It's awful that she's been hurt. There are so few left in the wild . . . '

'I know,' James agreed. 'But at least your mother's here and your father will be able to lend a hand, too. I'm sure they'll manage to find some way to help her.'

The cook came out, shaking her head at the uneaten food, which she put on a tray to take back to the kitchen. 'Please,' Mandy asked her, 'do you know what's happening?'

The cook shook her head.

'I don't think she speaks English,' James said.

Mandy walked to the window and stared out at the compound. Although it was empty, the lights in the other hut were lit and she could see people inside. James joined her. 'Let's go over,' he suggested. 'Maybe someone will be able to tell us what's going on.'

Mandy opened the door of the hut and was hit by a blast of bitter wind. 'It's freezing,' she muttered, as she went to get her jacket. Once they both had warm clothes on, they ran over to the research station and waited, teeth chattering, until

Mandy's knock was answered by the girl who had delivered the news about the sick panda.

The girl smiled shyly. 'Come in,' she said, 'I'm Mei Ling, by the way. Dr Yun's my mother.'

Mandy and James shook hands as they introduced themselves in turn. 'Do you know how the panda is?' Mandy asked.

Mei Ling shook her head. 'Not yet. I only know she is very ill. One of the workers called on the radio that he had found her wounded. I told my mother right away. It's good that Mrs Hope's here,' Mei Ling went on, as she led them along a passageway to a room filled with radio equipment, where Mr Chang was sitting at a receiver, talking in Chinese. 'We have a radio link with a vet at the Wolong Panda Conservation Centre. She has been helping Mrs Hope.'

Mandy held her breath as the rapid exchange in Chinese continued.

Mei Ling listened intently with a concerned expression on her face. Dr Yun's daughter was slim and about the same height as Mandy. She had short, very straight, dark hair and delicate features. As the exchange ended, she turned to Mandy and James. 'The treatment's been successful, the vet thinks,' she announced. 'They will all be back soon.'

'That's great news!' James exclaimed.

Mandy's relief was tempered by concern for the animal. The panda would have to survive the night in temperatures that were far below zero. 'Will the panda be safe outside in this weather?' she asked Mei Ling, thinking of the sick farm animals that her father sometimes treated in the comparative comfort of a barn.

Mei Ling smiled. 'Of course. She is under the shelter of the trees, and pandas have a thick, oily coat which keeps them warm and dry.'

'Your mother said that she was your oldest panda,' Mandy said worriedly.

Mei Ling nodded. Mr Chang turned off the radio and then they all walked back to the accommodation hut together. 'Li Li is about fifteen years old, we think. She wanders all over the place. We hadn't seen her for months, because she lost her tag.'

'All the pandas here have radio tags that give out signals,' Mr Chang explained. 'We can check their location with a receiver, so we know where they are.' He grinned broadly. 'Sometimes they lose their tags and then we have to hunt for them. Li Li has lost two tags, so Dr Yun decided not to tag her again, because the tags are quite expensive.'

Mandy and James smiled too. When they

reached the accommodation hut, the cook came out with some food, which Mei Ling and Mr Chang ate hungrily. Mandy watched the deft way that they used chopsticks, as easily as she used a knife and fork. She jumped up when she heard footsteps on the wooden veranda outside and dashed to the door to meet her mother.

'How's the patient?' she demanded, before Emily even had a chance to say hello.

Emily laughed despite the strain that was evident on her face. 'Li Li had a deep cut on her forepaw that had gone septic, so I gave her an antibiotic,' she said. 'We watched her for a while afterwards, and she seemed OK. She's listless, but that's only to be expected.'

Mandy sighed with relief.

'You haven't changed since I've been away!' Emily Hope said fondly, as she and the others took their places at the table and the cook brought out some more food for them. She turned to Adam. 'It was lucky that you'd arrived with the drugs I asked for.'

Adam Hope agreed. 'A strong antibiotic should do the trick.'

'I hope so. I got some advice from the vet at Wolong and then I darted her. I watched her for a bad reaction to the antibiotic, but she seemed OK.'

Mandy and James knew that wild animals

couldn't be treated like domestic pets; they had seen antibiotics and other drugs being administered by a dart gun when they had visited Africa. 'Won't the cut need to be cleaned and stitched?' Mandy asked.

'Let's hope not,' Emily said. 'To be stitched, she'd need a general anaesthetic, and that's very difficult to give to an animal in the wild. The vet at Wolong thinks it will heal without any more treatment, so long as the infection's been treated. Li Li's not far away, so we'll be able to go and have a look at her later.'

Mandy and James looked at each other. 'Don't even ask!' Mandy whispered, knowing that there was no way that they would be allowed to go with her mother. She didn't want to chance her luck so early in their stay.

'I'm relieved that you were here to help.' Dr Yun smiled. 'Li Li is special to me because she was the first panda I found when I came to work here.'

'How can you tell the pandas apart?' Mandy asked, fascinated.

'It takes time,' Dr Yun replied, 'but their markings are subtly different. The shades of the white portion of their coat vary. Also it is, what do you say, a process of elimination?'

Adam Hope nodded.

'We know there's a total of three adult females and one male,' Dr Yun went on, 'and we also know from the tags the location of the others, so when a tagless female appeared, it had to be Li Li! When I went to see her this morning, she was nowhere to be found. You can usually hear a panda crunching bamboo, because they spend most of the day eating, but I couldn't hear anything. I asked the workers to watch out for her and they found her, very listless with a visible wound. Fortunately, Emily was here to help.'

As the adults ate, Mandy turned to Mei Ling. 'Have you always lived here?' she asked.

'No. My mother and father used to work together at Wolong. Four years ago, my mother came here to study wild pandas,' she replied, in slow but very good English. 'That's her speciality, you see. She spends most of her time here, and the rest with my father at Wolong. Because the panda population here is too small to survive, we must move the pandas to the reservation. The corridor is nearly ready now. We hope the pandas will move this spring.'

Mei Ling got up and headed for the map on the wall, followed by Mandy and James. 'We are here,' she told them, pointing to a dot at the beginning of a thin red line and then tracing the line towards a larger dot. 'This is the Wolong reserve. It's many miles away, but as long as there is enough food along the way, we should manage to persuade the pandas to travel there. The workers have spent the last two years making sure there's plenty of bamboo along the trail, so this spring, once the pandas have mated, we will begin to move them in the right direction. They should arrive at Wolong by early summer.'

'You can't just move them in a truck or something?' James asked hopefully.

Mei Ling shook her head firmly. 'It would disturb them too much.'

Mandy gazed at the pictures of pandas that were pinned to the wall next to the map. She could not read the captions, which were written in Chinese.

Mei Ling smiled. 'These are our pandas,' she explained. 'These three are the females, Dong Dong, Su Lin and Li Li. The larger one is Mao Mao – the only male. We do not have pictures of the cubs yet. It is very important not to disturb the mother pandas when the cubs are very young.'

'How come there's only one male?' James queried.

Mei Ling shrugged. 'It's because the male panda always has a much larger territory than the female. Mao Mao is about eight years old, and he will chase

any other males away. Pandas leave their mothers when they are about eighteen months old. When Dong Dong's male cub left her we had to move him to Wolong because Mao Mao was threatening him. Pandas are very set in their ways, but if we are to stop them becoming extinct we have to give them a helping hand.'

James and Mandy were deep in thought as they returned to the table, where the others had just finished eating. Rick McGinley stood up and began to clear the table.

'Can we help?' James offered.

Rick grinned jovially. 'Here at the station we all

take turns to do the work. It's my turn today but yours will come soon enough.'

Dr Yun indicated the chair next to her. 'Come and join us,' she suggested, as Mr Chang explained that the workers would take turns to watch over Li Li throughout the night, in case the panda's recovery did not continue smoothly.

When the conversation turned to the health of wild pandas in general, though Mandy was fascinated, she couldn't suppress a yawn. At last, the long journey was catching up on her. 'I'm sorry,' she apologised, 'I don't mean to be rude.'

'Nonsense!' Dr Yun said firmly. 'You must all be exhausted. You've travelled so far and across so many time zones. It will be, what, early morning in England now? You and James must get some rest so that you're not too tired tomorrow.'

Emily and Adam Hope nodded vigorously in agreement as James hid a yawn behind a hastily raised hand.

'Can we see Li Li tomorrow?' Mandy asked hopefully.

'Don't worry,' Dr Yun smiled. 'You're going to see more than one panda over the next few days!'

Once she was in bed, Mandy couldn't help thinking about the injured panda in the bitter cold outside.

Along the wooden hallway, she heard the sounds of her mother and father leaving with Dr Yun and Rick. The thin blind over the window left a gap at the bottom, and she could see big flakes of falling snow.

'Mandy, are you asleep?' James hissed from behind the curtain that made his sleeping cubicle.

'No,' she replied. 'I'm worried about Li Li.'

'So am I,' James whispered.

'It's freezing outside.'

'I know, but remember what Mei Ling told us? Li Li's wearing the equivalent of a thick blanket with a waterproof jacket on top.'

'Mmm,' Mandy murmured. 'But if she's got an infection, she might have a fever. I'm worried that she's uncomfortable.'

There was a moment's silence as James thought about it. 'She'd be feeling much worse if your mum hadn't given her the antibiotic, wouldn't she?'

'Yes,' Mandy agreed.

'So we have done something to help,' James argued optimistically.

Their whispered conversation stopped as they heard the sounds of Emily and Dr Yun coming in again. Mandy waited, her heart thudding. After a moment, she got up, put on her dressing-gown and padded along the passageway. Her mother,

Dr Yun and Rick were drinking tea whilst Adam Hope was dozing in a seat besides the stove.

'How's Li Li?' Mandy asked urgently.

Emily's smile told her the answer. 'She's a little better, Mandy. The drug I gave her seems to be working.'

'She's sleeping comfortably,' Dr Yun added.

Adam Hope opened one eye. 'That's exactly what you should be doing!' he said.

'All right,' Mandy said, 'and I'll let James know there's nothing to worry about.'

Feeling a bit better, Mandy went back to her cubicle. Once she'd told James the good news, she got into bed.

Her last thought as she dozed off, now that she knew Li Li was going to be all right, was the memory of the surprised little black-and-white panda face staring at her through the bamboo leaves. She could hardly wait until the morning and a chance to get another glimpse of the cub.

Three

'Mandy, Mandy!'

Mandy opened one eye groggily. James was calling her from outside her cubicle.

Mandy glanced at her watch and sat up, appalled. It was already half past ten in the morning; she had slept much longer than she had intended to.

'I'll be there in a minute,' she said, jumping out of the bunk. She washed hurriedly in cold water in the makeshift bathroom and then pulled on woollen leggings and a vest, with jeans and a sweater on top. James was waiting in the common room, where the cook served them tea with rice and vegetable soup and sweet, doughy rolls.

'This is good!' James exclaimed, as he tore off a large chunk of roll. 'It certainly beats cereal and milk.'

'Mmm,' Mandy replied; she was too busy eating to answer him. For once, her excitement didn't spoil her appetite.

'I've already seen Rick this morning. He said he'd show us around later,' James told her, as he finished one roll and reached for another one.

Mandy grinned. 'Where are Mum and Dad?'

'They left a message with Rick that they've gone to see Li Li. I slept late myself,' James confessed. 'Rick says we're to go across to the research station when we're ready.'

Mandy frowned. Finding out how the sick panda was this morning was the first thing she wanted to do.

As they walked over to the research station, they heard Emily Hope's voice. Mandy and James hurried towards it, finding Emily and Adam just inside the door, along with Dr Yun and Rick.

'How's Li Li?' Mandy asked immediately.

Everyone smiled broadly. 'She's still a bit dopey, but she's definitely on the mend,' Emily confirmed.

'That's great!' Mandy said.

'I was just going to see her,' Dr Yun said. 'She's probably not up to fending for herself yet, so I thought I'd take her some breakfast. Would you like to come?'

'Yes please!' Mandy and James replied.

As they walked along the narrow path together, Dr Yun's daughter, Mei Ling, ran to join them. 'Do you live here all year round?' James asked her.

'Yes, at the moment,' Mei Ling replied, smiling. 'I attend the school in the village, but this year I am going to senior school in Wolong and will live with my father at the panda centre although we will spend our holidays here.'

'My husband works on the captive breeding programme,' Dr Yun explained. She smiled. 'Our work forces us to live apart, but we come together as a family as often as we can.'

As they walked deeper into the forest, the pine trees gave way to bamboo. The trees grew tall and straight, the evergreen leaves forming a canopy against the winter sun. Although the bamboo along the path was untouched, through the narrow trunks Mandy and James could see patches where leaves and stems had been torn away.

'The panda's appetite is voracious,' Dr Yun said,

'but you probably know that already.'

Mandy and James nodded. 'Mr Chang told us.'

'Fortunately, bamboo grows very quickly,' the zoologist continued, 'so there is still enough for the local people to use for handicrafts. You'll see them when you go down to the village.'

'I read that the bamboo died a few years ago,' Mandy remarked.

The zoologist frowned. 'Yes, the bamboo flowered and bamboo plants die after they flower. It happens only rarely, but it was very sad. There wasn't enough food for the wild pandas, and many starved.'

Mandy shivered and James's cheerful expression vanished.

Dr Yun pointed to a bamboo plant that looked different from the others. 'That's why we're planting various different species of bamboo. You see, only one species flowers at once and so there will always be food for the pandas that way.'

'Why do you think pandas eat only bamboo?' Mandy asked her.

Dr Yun smiled. 'That's a long story, Mandy. The short answer is that we're not sure. Actually, they can eat more or less anything, but in the wild ninety-nine per cent of their diet is bamboo.'

'So they just like bamboo?' James suggested.

Dr Yun nodded, then continued. 'In ancient times, pandas were hunted for their pelts, so perhaps man drove them into the high bamboo forest to hide, and they had to eat bamboo to survive. It's been that way for a long time – their jaw muscles are specially developed for a diet of bamboo and so is their gut.'

The sound of footsteps behind them heralded the arrival of Rick, who was carrying a large basket covered with paper. 'Rice balls,' he explained. 'Freshly made by Cook.'

Mandy smiled.

As the path approached a bend, Dr Yun slowed down and held her finger to her lips. 'Li Li is in a clearing just beyond this thicket,' she whispered. 'I don't want to startle her with too much noise.'

The zoologist walked forward very slowly with Rick and Mandy; James and Mei Ling followed behind. Mandy's heart was thudding at the prospect of seeing the panda. She could tell by the tense expression on James's face that he was excited too.

Dr Yun stood on tiptoe and peered through the bamboo, then she beckoned for the others to join her. Mandy crept forward, holding her breath. On

the far side of the clearing she saw a panda sitting down chewing slowly on a bamboo stem. Mandy was speechless.

'It looks like the antibiotics worked,' James whispered.

'It does,' Dr Yun agreed. 'Li Li's still very listless, but she's certainly improving. With her sore forepaw, she'll find it difficult to get all the bamboo she needs, so we'll leave these rice balls in case she gets hungry.' She took the basket of rice balls from Rick and, very slowly, walked straight up to the panda.

Li Li gazed at her with a puzzled expression on her chubby face, but clearly she was not frightened. When Dr Yun was within two metres of Li Li, she uncovered the basket and left it there, and walked slowly back to the others.

They all watched with bated breath as the panda gazed at the basket. Li Li's infected forepaw was swollen, but she didn't seem unduly bothered by it. 'Emily says it looks better than it did yesterday,' Dr Yun said, softly.

Very slowly, Li Li took a cautious step forward, holding her sore forepaw off the ground. She looked round and then sniffed at the rice balls. Once she had sniffed, she shifted forward clumsily and then plonked down on her rear. She looked round again before she picked up a rice ball and began to chew at it.

Mandy was thrilled. 'Isn't she wonderful?' she said to James, who was watching, intrigued. Rick was smiling to himself.

'It's fantastic to see a panda so close,' James said, shaking his head in amazement. 'They're just incredible to watch. Their coats are so distinctive. Lots of other wild animals are hard to see in the wild.'

Rick grinned. 'There's two theories about pandas' coats,' he explained. 'One is that because pandas are supposed to be antisocial animals, their highly distinctive markings help them to stay away from each other. The other is that the colouring helps them to find each other during the mating season.'

Mandy and James laughed.

Li Li had finished her first rice ball and was chewing a second one.

'We'd better leave her in peace now,' Dr Yun said.

Mandy looked at the panda for another moment and then, like the others, she crept away.

'We must be careful not to disturb Li Li while she's recovering,' Dr Yun remarked. 'It will take her a while to get her strength back and she is not used to strangers.'

Mandy nodded, deep in thought. 'Oh, by the way, we saw a cub yesterday – at least we think it was a cub – on our journey up here.'

'That's odd,' Dr Yun looked puzzled. 'How big was it?'

'We only saw its face, but it was about this high.' Mandy gestured with her hand to just below her knee.

'That would be a cub of three, four months old,' Dr Yun said thoughtfully. 'Are you sure that's what you saw?'

'Yes,' Mandy and James assured her.

Mei Ling looked puzzled. 'Where was it?'

'On the track below the research station,' James replied.

Dr Yun frowned and for a moment she and Mei Ling talked in Chinese. 'Excuse us,' Mei Ling said, 'we're just trying to work out which cub it could be. They usually never go anywhere near the track.'

'We know exactly where they are, because the mothers are radio-tagged,' Dr Yun explained. 'But we'll check when we get back to the office just to make sure.'

Mandy frowned too. 'We only saw it for a second,' she said, 'but it was definitely a cub.'

*　*　*

In the research station, Dr Yun checked the radio monitoring equipment. 'The mothers we know of are some distance away, higher up the mountain,' she said, as she studied the readings. 'Contact with humans disturbs nursing mothers, so we're careful to give them plenty of space until the cubs are weaned.'

'Could it be Li Li's cub?' Mandy wondered.

'Possibly. Li Li has been without a tag for many months now,' Dr Yun explained to Mandy and James. 'Maybe she's had a cub we just didn't know about.'

Rick was silent, but he looked concerned.

'It's possible,' Dr Yun said, thoughtfully. 'I suppose the cub could have wandered off and Li Li hurt herself when she was looking for it.' She strode out of the radio room to the office where Emily and Adam Hope were studying some research papers. The others followed her. 'Emily,' Dr Yun asked urgently. 'Did you know if Li Li was producing milk?'

Emily Hope brushed a strand of hair from her face. 'I don't know,' she replied. 'I couldn't get close enough to examine her. Why?'

'Mandy and James say they saw a cub on the track below the research station yesterday,' Dr Yun explained.

Emily Hope stood up. 'Are you sure?'

'I'm certain,' Mandy nodded solemnly.

Emily frowned. 'Li Li certainly couldn't have kept up with a cub yesterday. Her forepaw was far too sore for her to travel any distance. Could the cub have wandered off?'

Dr Yun was shaking her head. 'It would be unusual, but it might have done, I suppose. They're at the age when they're beginning to move around and play games.'

Mandy's heart lurched. 'Mum, could you have frightened the cub off when you treated Li Li?'

'I don't know,' Emily Hope said anxiously.

Dr Yun thought for a moment. 'It could have been one of the other cubs,' she said. 'In the winter, the pandas do come down the mountain to look for food.'

'I guess it's possible,' Rick agreed. 'But they would have moved away quickly as soon as they heard the Jeep.'

'But we both saw it,' James said quickly.

Rick nodded. 'OK,' he said, 'let's go and have a look for this cub of yours.'

Mandy and James followed as Rick strode down the rocky track. He moved fast, and they had to run to keep up with him.

'D'you think the cub could belong to Li Li?' Mandy panted, as she jogged alongside him.

'I don't know,' Rick said, sceptically. 'The cubs aren't weaned. They can't survive without their mothers.' He paused and turned to face them. 'Look, are you guys sure you saw a panda cub?'

Mandy and James exchanged a glance. 'Yes,' Mandy replied. 'Why are you asking?'

Rick rubbed his beard. 'It's just that you'd been travelling for more than a day and you both must have been jet-lagged. I was wondering if it could have been something else.'

'Like what?' James queried.

Rick shrugged. 'I don't know. A bit of white paper, or snow, or something. This is a big mountain, and there are only a few pandas on it. It's strange that you saw a cub where nobody's ever seen one before.'

Mandy shook her head slowly. 'It was definitely a panda. It was facing me. I saw the black patches round its eyes. The moment it noticed us, it disappeared.'

'I'm positive too!' James added.

'OK,' Rick agreed, reluctantly.

The track was covered with a thin layer of snow. In their wellington boots, Mandy and James had to concentrate on not slipping on the icy rocks. Rick wore hiking boots with thick soles that gripped the ground more firmly. Mandy could tell that he wasn't sure whether or not to believe them.

'Where exactly was it that you saw the cub?' Rick asked.

Mandy looked around. 'I think it was just round this bend, or maybe the next one,' she replied, as she looked up and down the track. She was trying to find something that she remembered, but it all looked the same to her.

James suddenly turned and began walking back up the hill. 'What are you doing, James?'

'We were coming upwards,' he replied. 'We've got a better chance of finding the place if we look at it that way.'

Mandy joined him. 'I think it was further down, round the next bend,' she said.

Rick was shaking his head slowly. 'The pandas never come down as far as this,' he emphasised. 'It's not far from the clearing where we found Li Li but the pandas never come anywhere near the track. Trucks terrify them.'

'I'm sure I saw it,' Mandy insisted.

Rick shrugged. 'OK, we'll give it another try. But only as far as the next bend. I mean, maybe you were day-dreaming or something like that.'

James shot an annoyed look at Mandy. She had to bite her tongue. As they rounded the bend, they saw a Chinese woman accompanied by a teenage boy. The woman was smaller than the boy but the skin of her face was heavily lined and the strand of hair that escaped her headscarf was grey. Despite the cold, she wore a thin cotton jacket and trousers and ragged fabric boots. The boy's clothes were similar and he was shaking his arms vigorously as if to ward off the cold. Both of them looked extremely worried.

Rick stopped and spoke to them in halting Chinese. The woman and boy looked at each other. Rick spoke to them again, even more slowly this time.

The woman gestured down the track and then said something to him.

Rick's frown deepened as he questioned her. He shook his head when the woman spoke. She began to gesture, and he looked at her intently and then asked her another question. Mandy noticed that the woman seemed to become agitated. When she gestured again, Rick turned and, without any explanation, began to run back up the track.

'What's happening now?' James asked, turning to Mandy.

'I don't know,' she said grimly. 'The only way we're going to find out is if we follow him.'

Four

Mandy and James couldn't keep up with Rick after the first bend and when they finally reached the research station Rick was standing with Adam and Emily Hope while Dr Yun was addressing all the workers in Chinese.

Mandy strode straight up to her mother. 'What's going on?'

Emily took her and James to one side. 'You were right,' she told them. 'There is a cub there. The people Rick spoke to saw it earlier this morning. Dr Yun's organising a search now.'

Mandy's heart was thudding. James's face had turned pale.

'The cub has to be reunited with Li Li urgently. Otherwise there's a danger she'll reject it,' Emily added.

Adam Hope nodded. 'Like so many wild animal mothers, pandas will reject a cub if it's handled by a human, so we've got to find it before anyone touches it!'

As the workers dispersed to search the mountainside, Rick joined them. 'I'm sorry I didn't believe you two,' he apologised. 'You see, it's just that I've been studying the pandas here for more than a year now, and I've never known any of the pandas to wander down so low.'

'Never mind. The important thing now is to find the cub and get it back to Li Li,' Mandy stated.

'That's right,' Rick agreed. 'We need your help to find the exact spot where you saw the panda. Once we know that, we can search properly.'

As Rick set off down the track for the second time that morning, Mei Ling joined Mandy and James. She carried a radio handset. 'When you find the place where you saw the cub, I'll tell the others,' she explained. 'It's a big area. We must all help.'

'We certainly will!' Mandy agreed. Her heart was pounding as she contemplated the threat to the cub.

Mei Ling moved closer to them. 'Rick's a nice

man,' she explained. 'My mother says he is a very good zoologist. But my mother also says that Rick gets on better with animals than with people!'

Mandy laughed. 'I know the type,' she said, thinking of Lydia Fawcett back in Welford, who preferred to stay up at High Cross Farm with her goats.

Mei Ling held her finger to her lips. 'We must be quiet now,' she whispered. 'We must not frighten the cub with too much noise.'

Ten minutes later, Mandy, James and Mei Ling stood together on the track. Mandy tried hard to recall exactly where she had seen the cub.

'I think it was near here,' James said softly.

Mandy closed her eyes and saw the little black-and-white face again. It had been about half a metre above the ground; she hadn't even seen the cub's full face, only its ears, eyes and nose between the thick green leaves of a bush. She opened her eyes again and looked around. The track beside her was lined with conifers, but a little lower down she saw a smaller bush that stood less than a metre tall.

With James and Mei Ling following, Mandy walked down past the bush and then turned and walked up again. She stood gazing at the bush for a moment. It matched her memory exactly, from the fragile lower stems to the bright green leaves that erupted from the top.

'This is it,' James said. 'I'm sure.'

Mandy nodded. 'Unless there's another bush like this lower down.'

Mei Ling shook her head. 'This is arrow bamboo,' she explained, in a whisper. 'It's a different species from Nan bamboo. This is the only arrow bamboo plant along the track – I know because I planted it last year to see if it would grow here.' She spoke rapidly into the radio set and then waited for an answer. Once it came, she nodded to herself. 'The others will come down to here,' she explained. 'The cub will not go far without its mother unless something makes it panic.' She smiled. 'It's lucky you saw it at the arrow bamboo, or we would have had great trouble finding it.'

Mandy peered into the undergrowth. 'We're quite a distance from where Li Li was found,' she pointed out.

'On the track, yes,' Mei Ling agreed, 'but not so far straight up the mountainside. Only about a hundred metres.'

'What do we do now?' James asked worriedly.

Mei Ling held a finger to her lips. 'Not so loud, else you will frighten the cub. We wait.'

'How long can the cub survive without its mother?' Mandy whispered.

Mei Ling's head tilted to one side as she pondered the question. 'Maybe a day or two. Maybe longer. It depends when it last fed.'

James gazed at Mandy. 'It's nearly twenty hours since we saw it,' he said softly.

Mandy's heart sank. Some distance down the track, Rick was walking up and down agitatedly.

'That's not the only problem,' Mei Ling whispered. 'A mother panda is likely to reject a young cub if they are separated for even a short time.' She went on. 'With an older cub, it can be away for hours, maybe longer. From the size of the panda you have described, it is not old enough to be separated. However, as Li Li is sick, maybe she doesn't know the cub is missing. If we get it back to her today, there is a chance.'

Neither Mandy nor James voiced the thought that came to them both at once. What would happen to the cub if it lost that chance?

Mei Ling's radio crackled. She answered the call and then switched it off. 'The other searchers are in position,' she explained in a murmur. 'Now we will walk very slowly back to the research station. If the cub is around here, we will find it!'

With thudding hearts, Mandy, James and Mei

Ling made their way cautiously up the track, taking great care with every step not to make any noise. Mandy and James searched each side of the track as Mei Ling walked up the middle, their eyes scanning all around.

Every ten metres or so, they stopped and checked the area they had just searched a second time. Mandy's stomach knotted as yet again she saw James and Mei Ling shake their heads.

'We must be getting close,' she murmured to herself, as she began to look even harder. Every time Mandy saw something white her heart nearly stopped, but each time it turned out to be a block of frozen snow.

When they paused next, James pointed to the sky, where the sun had already passed its midway mark and dark clouds were gathering. If the cub was to survive, it *had* to be found soon.

Way below them, Rick, his face taut with worry, was watching to make sure that the searchers did not drive the cub further down the mountainside. Every time they looked at him, he signalled that he'd seen no sign of it.

Mei Ling's expression was one of intense concentration, but underneath that, Mandy could sense her anxiety too. James was equally concerned.

Suddenly, Mandy saw a patch of white amidst the bamboo fronds. She stopped dead, afraid that it was again the remnants of a lump of snow fallen from a pine branch. But when she looked closer, she saw that there was something darker almost entirely hidden by the undergrowth. She leaned even closer, careful not to disturb the forest's stillness, and saw, under a clump of grass, the unmistakable shape of a young panda cub curled tightly into a ball.

Mandy's heart was in her mouth. For a moment, she was afraid that the cub was dead, then she noticed its abdomen move gently with the rhythm

of breathing. The cub was only sleeping!

Holding her finger to her lips, she beckoned James and Mei Ling, who tiptoed over. When he saw the panda cub, James waved his arms triumphantly. Mei Ling was so thrilled that she squeezed Mandy's hand.

Then, in silence, Mei Ling led them up the track. Once they were far enough away from the cub, she made a radio call for help.

'What now?' Mandy asked urgently.

'We have to move it very carefully,' Mei Ling explained. 'They will come with gloves and gowns, so the cub will not smell of humans. Well done, Mandy!'

James grinned. 'You've saved its life,' he cried.

Mandy's smile was tempered by doubt. 'Not just yet,' she cautioned him. 'We still have to get it safely back to Li Li.'

'At least it's got a chance now,' James insisted.

Rick arrived first, his hurried breath making misty trails in the thin mountain air. 'The others are on their way,' Mei Ling assured him. They were about fifty metres down from where they'd seen the sleeping cub, far enough away not to disturb it.

'Where is it?' Rick asked Mandy. Silently, she beckoned for him to follow her up the slope. The panda cub was still sleeping peacefully, its little forepaws against its ears as if it wanted some peace.

The huge zoologist bent down to take a closer look. Mandy was impressed with the way that he moved in absolute silence.

When Rick saw the panda cub, his face broke out in a smile. He watched for several minutes and then stood up again. Very slowly, they crept back to the others.

Rick shook his head. 'I'm so glad you found it,' he said softly. 'The cub must be hungry and missing its mother terribly. We'll have to get it back to Li Li as soon as we can.'

Mandy's joy at finding the cub was shadowed by the knowledge that its hardest obstacle was yet to come. If Li Li rejected the cub, what would happen to it? She suddenly remembered it hadn't eaten for nearly a whole day. 'Can we give the cub some food?' she asked Rick.

Rick shook his head vigorously. 'It might not have been weaned yet. Nobody has managed to hand-rear a panda cub, and, even if we *could* get it to eat, the chances are that it would never be able to return to the wild.'

Mandy's heart raced. 'So it has to go back to Li Li before it can eat?'

Rick nodded. 'That's right. But food isn't the only problem.'

'What's the other one?' James queried.

'The cub will pine terribly if Li Li rejects it. If she does, I don't know what we'll do.'

At last, a worker arrived from the research station with an assortment of sterile gowns, sheets and gloves. Rick took charge of the cub-moving operation. First of all, he took off his big down jacket and put on blue surgical scrub trousers over his jeans and then two surgical gowns on top of that. Deftly, Mei Ling secured the ties at the back of the gowns, while Rick put on surgical gloves, which he rubbed against some bamboo leaves before he put another pair on top. 'Better to be on the safe side,' he said.

Taking a green sterile wrap, he walked slowly towards the cub. Mandy, James and Mei Ling watched, but they did not follow for fear of disturbing the delicate procedure.

'Wouldn't Dr Yun be better carrying the cub?' James asked. 'I mean, surely she knows the pandas better.'

Mei Ling shook her head. 'My mother only studies wild pandas. Because of Rick's experience with pandas in captivity he knows how to lift them properly.'

Mandy and James watched as the zoologist came back carrying the cub wrapped in the sterile scrub. They gave Rick plenty of room to pass, then followed him back to the research station. It was now afternoon and the winter sun was about to disappear behind the mountains far to the west.

The chill in the air nipped Mandy's cheeks as the procession headed by Rick and the panda cub slowly moved up the mountainside, and she began to shiver. At last, they reached the research station where Dr Yun and Adam and Emily Hope were waiting anxiously.

Rick carried on walking towards the bamboo thicket where Li Li was still recovering from her infection, holding the cub in his arms. Dr Yun went ahead to check the mother panda's position – the others followed at a distance.

No one said a word.

A pitiful high-pitched wail came from the bundle in Rick's arms. Mandy winced but Mei Ling assured her that the sound was one that all young pandas made. 'Perhaps the cub knows it is near to its mother,' she whispered.

'I hope so!' Mandy agreed, fervently.

At the bamboo thicket, Dr Yun waved Rick forward. Despite his bulky form, the zoologist moved as nimbly and silently as the deer that

Mandy and James had seen the day before. Hardly a leaf fluttered in the big man's wake.

Through the greenery, Mandy could see Li Li. The panda was sitting chewing slowly at a bamboo stem; the basket of rice balls was completely empty.

'She's still very weak,' Emily Hope whispered, 'Often animals are confused when they're ill. We're hoping that Li Li won't realise how long it's been since she's seen her cub.'

Rick stopped about twenty metres way from Li Li. Hidden by a thick bamboo plant, he very tenderly put the cub down and then stepped away. 'It's a little boy, by the way,' he whispered to the others.

The cub looked round, as if puzzled. Li Li continued to chew her bamboo stem. They all watched with bated breath as the cub sat up and then, hesitantly, on all fours, made his way towards the female panda.

When he was within a few metres of Li Li, she noticed him. For a moment, she stopped chewing her bamboo stem.

The panda cub whimpered and then scratched his ear.

Mandy glanced at Rick, who was watching intently.

Li Li gazed at the cub; then an expression that

looked like a frown passed over the panda's chubby features.

The cub whimpered again and then, confused, turned round. Sniffing, he began to move around in a slow circle, wailing pitifully.

Rick muttered under his breath. Dr Yun's face was frozen.

The tension was too much for James. 'What's going on?' he asked.

Rick's face was grim. 'Li Li doesn't recognise the cub, and the cub certainly doesn't recognise her! The cub's not Li Li's,' he said, tersely.

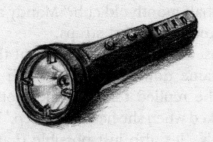

Five

'Can we help?' Mandy asked her father, as Dr Yun spoke urgently into her radio to call all the research station staff back to the clearing, where the search for the cub's real mother was about to begin.

'No' Adam replied firmly. 'It's getting late and it's freezing.'

Emily stood beside him, shaking her head. 'After you've had dinner, you two had better get to bed.'

Mandy frowned but she knew that it was pointless to argue.

Rick was filling his rucksack with a flask of hot tea and some chocolate bars he must have brought over from Canada, along with a strong torch and a radio set. 'Why would a mother panda abandon a four-and-a-half-month-old cub?' Mandy asked him, as he secured the pocket straps.

'The most likely explanation is that the mother and cub came down lower to search for better bamboo,' he replied tersely. 'The mother might have panicked when she heard the Jeep.' He paused thoughtfully. 'It's also just possible that when we collected the cub, thinking that he had been abandoned, he wasn't abandoned at all and the mother was somewhere nearby gathering bamboo.'

Mandy froze. 'So the cub would have been OK if we'd left it alone?'

'I don't know,' Rick grunted. 'The only way to find out is to locate the other two mothers so we can work out which one the cub belongs to. It's possible that the mother has been injured like Li Li. If she was, perhaps she panicked and lost her cub. I just don't know, Mandy. I've never heard of a cub of this age that's been found without its mother before.'

Mandy and James watched the research station workers preparing for the search for the missing mother panda. While some of them carried battery torches, others held old tin candle lamps. According to the radio tags, both mother pandas were higher up the snow-covered mountain, so away from the research station the workers would need as much light as possible.

Not long after Rick had departed, Adam Hope and two of the workers set off in the opposite direction to the one that he had taken. Emily was staying behind to monitor the radio. Dr Yun had called her husband for help with the search, but a heavy snowstorm in Wolong was going to make the journey difficult.

Mandy glanced at the night sky where the moon was shrouded by clouds. She shivered at the thought that, in these conditions, somewhere on the mountain, a mother panda was searching for her lost cub. The panda cub had been put into a hastily built pen just outside the research station, where Rick had assured her that he would be safe for the night.

'Let's go and have some dinner,' James suggested. 'It smells delicious!'

Frustrated, Mandy sat down at the table. James was ploughing his way through a huge bowlful of crispy Sichuan chicken and rice, but Mandy did not touch the stir-fried mushrooms with noodles that the cook had made especially for her. Mei Ling was pushing some rice round her bowl with her chopsticks.

'Why aren't you eating?' Mei Ling asked her.

Mandy put her bowl to one side. 'I'm just not hungry,' she replied, as she watched Mei Ling gracefully pick up the bowl and eat the rice. 'I can't get the hang of these chopsticks,' she added, trying to sound a bit more light-hearted.

Mei Ling smiled. 'I don't know how to eat with a knife and fork!' she retorted.

Despite her anxiety, Mandy giggled briefly.

'I'll show you how, if you like,' Mei Ling went on. 'You hold the chopsticks like this.'

Mandy watched the way the Chinese girl picked up both sticks and held one between her thumb and forefinger with the other resting between two fingers. 'You keep this one still and move the other one between your fingers,' Mei Ling said, as she demonstrated how to do it. 'It might look difficult, but once you know how, it's really simple.'

With great ease, she picked up a bit of pepper from a plate of vegetables and ate it. Then she smiled. 'That was a little rude of me,' she said. 'We use the spoons to put our food into the bowl, and then we use the chopsticks to eat it.'

Mandy tried very slowly to pick up a mushroom, but it slipped away from the chopsticks. 'How do you cope with rice and noodles?' James asked, taking his last mouthful.

Mei Ling laughed. 'That's why we use bowls to

eat. It means you can pick up the bowl with one hand, bring it close to your mouth, and use the chopsticks with the other hand.'

After a couple of tries, Mandy managed to eat a mushroom, but when she tried a noodle she dropped it on the table. 'I'm sorry,' she apologised.

Mei Ling shook her head. 'Don't be. It's nice that you're trying to learn to eat the Chinese way.'

'It looks like Mandy needs to stay up all night and practise!' James joked. Mandy smiled at her friend and then nudged him to get up and help Mei Ling clear the dishes away.

'It's awful to know a panda's in danger,' Mandy remarked, picking up a pile of bowls.

The Chinese girl nodded forlornly. 'The pandas are my friends.' She glanced at the wall, where the pictures of Dong Dong, Su Lin, Li Li and Mao Mao hung side by side. 'It's not nice to think that something's happened to one of them.'

Mandy murmured in agreement.

James blinked. 'At least the cub's going to be OK for another day or so. Rick says he's well fed and cared for.'

Mandy shook her head. 'But if his mother can't be found . . .'

'They will find the cub's mother,' Mei Ling asserted. 'The radio tag will show them where.'

Just then, Dr Yun appeared at the door. She spoke to Mei Ling in Chinese and then turned to Mandy and James. 'Emily's right,' she told them. 'Now you've eaten, it's time for all of you to go to bed.'

'We'd like to help,' Mandy pleaded.

'You've already helped by finding the cub,' Dr Yun smiled. 'You don't know the mountain, Mandy. It really is best if you leave it to us. I hope we'll have good news in the morning. Meanwhile, you must get some sleep.'

Reluctantly, the three of them went through to the cubicles at the back of the hut.

Mandy went to bed, but she could not sleep. She lay awake, thinking of the cub pining for his mother. Her travel clock showed that it was well after midnight, and there was still no sign of the missing panda. Mandy had been listening out nervously for any news.

'James?' she whispered.

'I'm awake,' he replied.

'So am I.' Mei Ling's voice came from the other side of the hallway. 'If I go over to the research station, I might be able to find out what's going on.'

'I'll come!' Mandy offered.

'I may as well go alone as they talk in Chinese. It's better if only one of us gets into trouble.'

Mandy nodded. She and James got up and followed Mei Ling to the door of the accommodation hut and watched as she crept across to the research station.

Mei Ling listened outside a window for several minutes before she came back. 'One mother is safe with her cub,' she told them, her teeth chattering as she stood shivering against the stove. 'Now they're looking for the other one.'

James padded into the kitchen to make Mei Ling some tea to warm her up. Suddenly, Mandy remembered the powdered chocolate drink she'd brought for her mum. She went to get it from her suitcase. 'Mei Ling,' she asked, 'have you ever had hot chocolate?'

Mei Ling shook her head. 'No, but Rick gave me chocolates for my birthday.'

'Would you like to try some?'

'Yes please!'

Mandy went to the kitchen, where she made hot chocolate for all three of them, then she and James joined Mei Ling at the stove. Mei Ling blew on the drink and then sipped it. 'Very sweet, but nice,' she smiled. 'Chocolate is my favourite taste.'

Mandy was thinking of the cub that was

separated from his mother. 'I wish we could do something to cheer up the cub,' she said.

Mei Ling shook her head. 'The only thing to do is to find his mother.'

'When will that be?' James asked as Mandy sighed sadly.

'Su Lin is about one thousand metres up the mountain,' Mei Ling told him. 'The snow is deep, and pandas sleep in a nest, a hollow in a tree or by a rock. The searchers think that they will not find the panda until tomorrow.'

Mandy glanced outside the window, where the wind was howling. The glass shook in the rickety frame. Although she knew that the baby panda had enough shelter, her heart ached for him.

'Will the searchers be all right?' James asked, anxiously.

'Yes,' Mei Ling said. 'They know this mountain and Rick is an experienced mountaineer.'

'What about Mandy's dad?' James asked.

'He's coming back soon, I think.'

Mandy's mind was spinning. There was a thought at the back of it that just wasn't clear. The area around the research station was vast. The maps on the wall showed that the mountain was nearly 3,500 metres high; at 1,050 metres, the research station had been built below the normal panda habitat so that the animals would not be disturbed by it. There was about ten square kilometres of territory above the station, and as much again below it.

She walked over to where the map was pinned to the wall and checked her calculations. 'A panda's home territory is, what, four to six square kilometres?' she remarked.

'Yes,' Mei Ling agreed. 'That's a male's territory. With each male's territory, there will be several females.'

'There's only three females and one male here,' Mandy continued.

'Yes, Mao Mao,' Mei Ling confirmed.

James's interest quickened. 'What are you thinking?' he asked Mandy.

Mandy's frown deepened. 'I'm just wondering if there could be another panda here that Dr Yun doesn't know about. There's enough room for another male, so there must be room for at least one more female.'

Mei Ling shook her head vigorously. 'That couldn't be. My mother has been here for several years. She knows all the pandas.'

James sat up. 'But there *is* room for another panda, isn't there?'

Mei Ling thought about it. 'There is in theory, but I'm certain there isn't another panda. They're not only radio-tagged – in the summer the workers also search for their nests and count their droppings.'

'Isn't it possible they missed one?' James asked.

Mei Ling sighed. 'It's always possible, but I don't think it's likely. My mother knows a great deal about pandas in the wild, and the people who work here have searched the mountain very carefully. But then again . . .' Her voice tailed off as she considered something.

'What is it?' Mandy asked.

Mei Ling looked doubtful. 'When my mother found out Su Lin and Dong Dong were going to have cubs, she told the workers to be careful not to disturb them. After the cubs were born she would not allow anyone to go near them.'

James and Mandy looked at each other. 'So how did you know the cubs were born?'

Mei Ling smiled. 'The pandas know my mother. They are not frightened of her. She was able to go close enough to make sure that the mothers and cubs were safe, and then she left them alone.' She shook her head. 'When my mother came here, at first she thought there was only one old female, and Mao Mao, who was two years old then. The female had two cubs before she died – Dong Dong and Su Lin. My mother found Li Li three years later. She told me she was not sure if Li Li had been here all the time or if she had come from somewhere else.'

Mandy's heart was racing.

'It was not long after the bamboo flowered and died,' Mei Ling explained. 'So many of the wild pandas had starved and the few who were left were very hard to find. It was long before we began to use radio tags. From a distance, it's easy to see a panda and assume it's one that you know.'

'So it's possible that there could be another female that your mother doesn't know about?' Mandy asked urgently.

Mei Ling thought hard before she answered. 'I suppose so. My mother says that the most important thing is not to disturb the pandas and, because she insists that each panda has plenty of space, it could be that there is one that hasn't been discovered yet.'

'If the other mother was lower down the mountain, she could have hurt herself too!' James finished.

Mei Ling stood up and began to pace the room. 'That makes sense,' she said. 'It makes as much sense as looking for Su Lin.' She stopped pacing. 'Without a radio tag, it won't be easy to find the panda. It won't be possible until the morning.'

The sounds of footsteps outside heralded the arrival of Rick McGinley and Adam Hope.

As the door burst open, Mandy flew over to her father. 'Dad,' she cried. 'You've got to listen to this! We think the cub might belong to another panda!'

Adam Hope frowned. 'What are you doing up at this time of the night?'

'We couldn't sleep because we were worried about the panda,' Mandy explained breathlessly. 'We've got an idea.'

Mei Ling nodded. 'Please listen, Mr Hope. It's the only thing that makes any sense.'

Mandy's dad paused for a moment. 'OK,' he agreed reluctantly, 'let's hear it, then.'

Rick paced the common room from end to end. Emily Hope stood with Dr Yun beside the stove as Mandy finished explaining her theory. Once he had heard what Mandy had to say, her dad had insisted on calling the others. When she stopped talking, there was silence for a moment. Mandy bit her lip as she waited impatiently.

'You might be right,' Dr Yun said, nodding. 'It's a possibility.'

Rick's loud voice boomed from the other end of the room. 'We should cover the options. We'll start the search at first light,' he announced. 'There's no point in starting now.'

Dr Yun agreed. 'If the panda is injured, there's a risk that we might frighten her. She might flee and we'd have little or no chance of finding her in the dark. I'm going to radio Wolong again right now. They might be able to send more people by daybreak.'

Mandy's heart was drumming with a mixture of fear and excitement as she thought of the hunt for the missing panda.

'It's a vast area,' Adam Hope pointed out.

'We have to try!' Mandy insisted passionately.

'Can we help you tomorrow?' James asked.

'We'll need as much help as we can get,' Rick assured him.

Emily Hope stood up. 'Nothing's going to happen before dawn,' she said firmly. 'We should all go to bed.'

'Will you promise to wake us first thing?' Mandy asked her mother.

Emily smiled tiredly. 'Of course we will.'

Mandy woke up at dawn as her mum gently shook her shoulder. She got out of bed immediately and dressed hurriedly in several layers of clothes. Thick frost on the window told her that it was terribly cold outside.

The cook was serving breakfast as Mandy joined a sleepy Mei Ling and James in the common room. Dr Yun and Rick were planning the search as they ate.

Mandy was too excited to eat more than a sweet roll. She sipped fragrant hot tea slowly as she listened to the conversation.

'There's a team coming from Wolong,' Dr Yun was saying, 'but they won't get here until this afternoon at the earliest.'

Rick shook his head. 'We'll have to do the best we can without them. Is there any chance of a helicopter?'

'Not with the weather like this,' Dr Yun said. 'The nearest heliport is storm-bound.'

Rick went to the window and glared at the sky. 'If it gets any worse, we'll lose the radio link with Wolong.'

James and Mandy exchanged worried glances.

Once everyone had finished eating breakfast, Dr Yun spread a large map of the mountain over the table. The research station workers were organised into teams of two and with a pencil the zoologist traced the route that each pair would take. Whilst the teams were making their final preparations, Mandy, James and Mei Ling waited impatiently to be told what they could do to help.

Dr Yun smiled distantly. She looked tired and also very worried. Mandy's eyes followed the route she traced on the map. 'This is an old yak trail,' the zoologist explained. 'It hasn't been used for years, but there's still a path of sorts there. What I want you to do is to take a radio and go right down the track to the trail, and then follow the yak trail back up to here. Mei Ling will go with you. She knows how to use the radio.

'Remember, what we're looking for is any sign of a deer trap, or any unusual disturbance in the undergrowth. Pandas are large animals but they're surprisingly nimble. If you notice that the leaves have been torn or the plants have been damaged, that might mean that an injured panda has been trying to find her way back to her cub. The way we normally find pandas in the wild is by looking for their droppings and then tracing them back to their rest sites. So keep a look out for droppings too.'

'Isn't the mother likely to be somewhere near where we found the cub?' James asked.

'That's our starting point,' Rick responded, 'but we've got to assume that the mother got injured and then the cub got lost. The cub's probably too young to have developed the senses that would enable him to find his mother on his own, but he's old enough to wander off playfully.' The big man's face took on a look of sadness. 'It seems the little one got carried away and when he looked round he discovered his mother wasn't there. Because his sense of location is not established yet, he could have wandered for as little as a hundred metres. Or as much as a kilometre.'

Mandy's heart ached for the panda cub.

Mei Ling put on her jacket and then slung a rucksack that contained the radio set over her shoulder. 'OK,' she said, 'let's go.' As they left, Mandy glanced at the thermometer that hung on the outside wall. The reading was ten degrees below zero.

For a while, none of them spoke. They were all thinking of the injured panda and her pining cub. Mandy was struggling against the fear that the panda mother was dead. It was now nearly forty hours since they had first seen the lone panda cub.

Mei Ling saw Mandy's troubled look. 'Don't think the worst,' she said, gently. 'Maybe the first time you saw the cub, the mother was OK. Maybe the mother was injured yesterday morning. Mrs Hope is a very good vet, my mother says. If we find the panda, Mrs Hope will save her.'

An icy wind blew up from the valley as Mandy wished that she could believe what Mei Ling had just said.

'What do you do when Mandy's mum isn't around?' James asked Mei Ling practically.

She shrugged. 'It's very unusual for a panda to get hurt. It's only happened once since my mother has been here and then she managed to get help from one of the vets at Wolong. But now that we are almost ready to move the pandas, my mother wanted Emily to come here to make sure that they were all healthy enough.'

The yak trail was much narrower that the track, following a roller-coaster path along the mountain-side.

Suddenly, Mandy heard a rustle in the under-growth. She stopped dead, her heart beating wildly.

'What's that?' James hissed in her ear, just as the Chinese boy they'd seen yesterday with the old woman appeared about fifty metres farther up the track.

'Hey!' Mandy cried, but the Chinese boy ignored her. The moment he saw them, he turned round and fled.

Six

'We have to find him,' Mei Ling panted. She had chased the Chinese boy along the trail with Mandy and James, but they had lost him.

Mandy frowned. 'Why did he run away like that?'

Mei Ling's face was sad. 'The village people are very poor. In winter, they have to trap deer because they're hungry. Maybe that boy left the trap that hurt Li Li. He will be terrified of getting caught.'

'But if it was him, it will have been an accident,' James protested. 'You can't blame him for trying to feed himself.'

Mei Ling nodded. 'He's at school with me. His

name is Tai An. Tai An's father died five years ago and it is the responsibility of Tai An and his mother to support both his father's and his mother's parents. In Chinese culture, it is an honour to care for our elders. It's very difficult for Tai An because he is at school and can't work and his mother is not well. The family are all very poor.'

Mandy nodded sympathetically. Despite her anger about the harm the boy might have caused the pandas, she understood that in the Chinese countryside there was a lot of hardship.

'If the government catch Tai An setting traps,' Mei Ling said breathlessly, 'maybe they will put him in jail. Many of the village people like Tai An, but some are jealous, because he is cleverer than their sons.'

'I see,' Mandy said. She felt sympathy towards the Chinese boy but was impatient to find the mother panda.

'The only thing to try is the old steps on the side of the mountain. If we go down them, maybe we will meet Tai An before he disappears.' Mei Ling paused to catch her breath. 'Tai An speaks English very well. If you follow him, he might trust you. Perhaps he is frightened of me because my mother is an important official.'

'Where are the steps?' Mandy demanded.

'I'll show you.'

Mei Ling set off running. Mandy and James raced after her, but she was quick on her feet and it was a struggle to keep up. Mandy had a stitch in her side by the time Mei Ling stopped at the uprooted trunk of a pine tree.

'Here.' She pointed to a steep drop of about one metre, followed by a ledge before another drop.

James squinted. 'You call these steps?'

Mei Ling nodded. 'In old times, people used to climb the mountain to hunt. Rather than carry the prey all the way down the yak trail, it was quicker to drop it down the steps.'

'Come on!' Mandy urged her friend, as she lowered herself down the first of the steps.

'Be careful!' Mei Ling cried after her. 'The steps meet the yak trail just above the village. If you hurry, you will find Tai An!'

'If we don't break our legs first,' James muttered.

'Come on!' Mandy insisted. 'There's no time to lose.'

After a while, Mandy and James got used to the steep steps carved into the rock of the mountain, although it was hard going because of slippery moss and branches of conifers and bamboo plants that obstructed their way. They found that they could use the branches for support and made good progress – until James lost his grip on a frosty branch of pine and slipped. Mandy dived to his rescue but she landed hard, jarring her knee.

'Sorry,' James apologised.

'It doesn't matter,' she winced, determined to ignore the pain. She was more concerned with their search for Tai An. Ten minutes later, she saw a dark blue shape moving through the thick foliage of the evergreens.

Mandy stopped dead. 'Shh,' she whispered, putting a finger to her lips. James froze. About fifty metres below, they could see Tai An quite clearly. He was moving down the steps slowly, pausing on each one to look in both directions.

Holding her breath, Mandy carefully descended a couple of steps. When she was three steps above Tai An, she whispered to James to wait for her. Then, very cautiously, she slipped down the steps until she was standing on the one where Tai An had just disappeared into the undergrowth. Mandy stood in silence, not wanting to startle the Chinese boy. She waited until he turned and saw her.

Tai An's eyes widened in fear. As he tried to make a run for it, Mandy grabbed his arm. Although he was bigger than her, she managed to keep her grip. 'Please, Tai An,' she pleaded, 'listen to me. I'm

from England, I'm nothing to do with the Chinese authorities and I won't tell anyone about this, I promise you.'

Tai An was trembling under his thin cotton jacket.

'Believe me, I won't do anything to harm you,' Mandy went on. 'I just need your help. We think a panda's been hurt in a deer trap. I know you speak English. Please – talk to me.'

Still Tai An's eyes were like dark saucers, full of mistrust.

Mandy thought for a moment. 'I know you wouldn't want to hurt a panda,' she beseeched him, 'but there's an injured panda mother out here somewhere and we have to find her to save her life and her cub's.'

Tai An blinked. 'I did not set a trap for a panda,' he said, very slowly. He shook his head vigorously. 'I would never do that.'

The look in his eyes made Mandy want to trust him. 'I know you wouldn't,' she said, letting go of his arm.

'My deer traps are always below the research station,' he said, 'never above. Dr Yun says the pandas stay above the station.'

'Yes,' Mandy agreed, 'but this year's been very cold. We already know that one panda came down to below the level of the research station. That panda *was* hurt by a deer trap.'

Tai An shook his head vigorously. 'Many people set deer trap. I am very careful.'

'Of course,' Mandy comforted him. She could tell that the Chinese boy was terrified. With a shudder, she remembered reading that the penalty for trapping a panda in China was imprisonment for life. 'I promise you, Tai An, nobody will blame you.'

Tai An said nothing.

Mandy's mind whirled. She had to find some way of getting Tai An to help. She thought very carefully before she spoke again. 'Tai An, you know the mountain very well, don't you?'

'Lower part, yes,' he agreed grudgingly. 'I never go near the research station.'

'We have to find the panda.'

Tai All nodded. 'I understand.'

'My mother is a vet. If we can find the injured panda, my mother will treat her,' Mandy said emphatically. 'I hope she will save her life and if she can, she will also save the life of the cub.'

'I saw the cub yesterday,' Tai An told her. 'I told the Canadian man. He ran away.'

'Yes, I know. We're all very worried about the cub and his mother,' Mandy explained. 'If you help us to find the mother panda, we'll be very grateful to you.'

Tai An looked away. Mandy could tell that he was thinking. She glanced at James, who had been listening carefully.

It seemed to Mandy that Tai An thought for a very long time. Her heart pounded as she waited for his answer. She knew that if he ran away again, he would make sure that it was very difficult for her and James to find him.

'It's only me that has talked to you,' she tried to persuade him. 'I'm not going to tell anyone about it. All I want to do is to find the missing panda.'

Tai An thought for a moment longer and then finally he nodded. 'OK,' he said, 'I will try to help. Only you must promise not to tell Dr Yun or anyone else, not even Mei Ling.'

'I promise,' Mandy agreed. She turned to ask James to tell Mei Ling to stay well away from Tai An, but James was already clambering to the steps. Mandy sighed in relief. The panda cub now had a chance, even if it was a slim one.

Tan An helped Mandy to scramble back up the steps. The Chinese boy was lithe and climbed easily, pausing at every step to give Mandy a hand.

When they rejoined the yak trail, they paused for breath.

'The steps are only meant for going downwards,' Tai An smiled. 'Not for climbing up again.' He set off along the trail with Mandy following. She felt glad that Mei Ling was nowhere to be seen.

'I will tell the truth now,' Tan An confessed. 'I set three traps. I normally set only one, but the harvest was bad this year and everyone is hungry, so many deer traps have been set. I set the traps in the forest two days ago and returned often to check them.' He shook his head. 'I hate setting traps. I prefer to hunt for deer, but my mother says there is more risk of being caught.'

Mandy returned his wistful smile. Although she would never hunt or trap an animal herself, she had travelled to parts of the world where she knew that the people had to kill animals to feed themselves.

'I understand that people have to eat,' she assured him.

Tai An had slowed his pace so that she could keep up with him. 'You speak English very well,' Mandy said.

He put his hands in his pockets. 'I work hard at school. I hope I will be able to go to university.' He smiled thinly. 'Maybe I will become a veterinary surgeon like your mother. Although I have to kill deer to survive I like animals very much. I think, sometimes, animals are preferable to people.'

'I think so too,' Mandy agreed.

Tai An looked away. 'In China, everyone is supposed to be equal,' he said, slowly. 'But sometimes the privileges are not shared equally by all.'

Mandy nodded understandingly. 'Every part of the world has its problems. The West is not all movies and hamburger restaurants,' she responded carefully.

Tai An laughed. 'I have listened to the BBC World Service on the radio and I would like to visit England one day.'

'I hope you will,' Mandy said warmly. She liked the good-natured Chinese boy.

They were nearing the beginning of the old yak trail when she heard the sound of footsteps. She turned and saw James running to catch up with them.

'Tai An, this is my friend James.' She introduced them, and the two boys nodded in acknowledgement.

'OK,' Tai An said, getting back to the point. 'Early yesterday morning, I returned to the three traps I had set, but I found only two. When I heard that a panda had been hurt, I went to my mother for help. I saw the cub on my way. My mother came with me to apologise for setting the trap, but the Canadian man ran away before I had a chance to explain. I do not think he understood what we were saying. I did try to find the third trap, but I could not. When I saw you two, I was afraid. That's why I ran away. I am sorry. I will try to help you now.'

'Where did you leave the trap?' James asked.

Tai An pointed into the forest. 'I thought it was at the foot of that pine tree. It is not close to bamboo so there was no danger to the pandas. I went to find the trap again today, but when I realised the station workers were searching the mountain, I got scared and turned to go home.'

Tai An led the way into the trees with Mandy and James following. The undergrowth was thick but Tai An deftly cleared a path for them. The morning sun was melting the frost and snow on the branches, and icy water dripped down their necks from the icicles that hung from the pines. None of them spoke of any discomfort; Mandy could feel her knee beginning to swell but she could still walk and she was sure it was only a sprain. She knew that the important thing was to find the deer trap and then at least they would have a clue as to where the mother panda might be.

Tai An showed them a slight mark in the hard earth. 'The trap was just here,' he said.

Mandy and James peered at the frozen ground. They could see nothing that suggested what had happened to the trap.

'Could a deer have run away with it?' James asked hopefully.

Tai An shook his head. He looked away. 'The trap would cut through the deer's leg. The deer would bleed to death shortly afterwards.'

Mandy felt sick at the thought of an animal suffering so badly.

James's face was white. 'Would the trap cut off a panda's leg?' he queried tremulously.

'No, it would only break the skin. A panda's coat is much thicker than a deer's, so the coat protects the panda. Also, the panda's rear leg is much bigger than a deer's, so the trap cannot shut.'

'We have to find that trap,' Mandy said grimly.

They began to search the undergrowth carefully. The trap was made of metal, Tai An told them; it was a semi-circular device with a radius of about fifteen centimetres.

Mandy struggled to concentrate. Her limbs were tired after the exertion of climbing the steps and her knee had begun to throb, but her concern for the panda and the cub that was pining for his mother drove her on.

'Remember, we've got to look out for panda droppings,' James pointed out.

Tai An smiled patiently. 'I'm sure he knows that,' Mandy whispered to James.

After a while, she heard James stumble. 'Ouch! ' he cried, as a broken pine branch gouged a gash in his cheek. Mandy and Tai An rushed over to help him up. 'I'm OK,' he insisted, as Mandy tried to stop the bleeding with a tissue.

'Let's carry on then,' she said, pulling James to his feet.

Mandy bit her lip. She'd had many adventures at Animal Ark, but the mountainous Chinese countryside was nothing like the small Yorkshire village where she lived. As her eyes scanned the ground for the metal trap, she began to give up hope of ever finding it.

'Wait!' James's face was like a ghost's as he pointed to a twisted and rusted bit of metal that was barely visible under a branch of bamboo that was heavily laden with snow. 'That's it, isn't it?' James said, tremulously.

Tai An blinked. Although the Chinese boy's face seemed expressionless, Mandy could sense that beneath the bland expression he tried to maintain there was a mixture of both worry and great shame.

'Yes,' Tai An confirmed sadly. 'I'm afraid it is.'

Mandy gulped as she saw the dark stain in the earth below the trap, along with a clump of white panda fur.

Seven

'Go!' Mandy told the trembling Tai An.

He hesitated. 'Perhaps I can still help . . .'

Mandy glanced at the forest beyond the place where they had found the trap. The undergrowth had been disturbed, as Dr Yun had said it would be. She was sure that the mother panda was not far away.

She shook her head. 'You've helped enough already. Now we know where the panda is, we'll have to radio the workers to help.'

'I'm very sorry.' Tai An's head hung in shame.

'I know, and don't worry, I'll keep my promise,' Mandy said firmly.

Tai An turned to leave. A moment later, he had vanished into the depths of the forest. Mandy turned to James. 'Where's Mei Ling?'

'She said she'd follow out of sight.'

'Go and find her,' Mandy told him. 'Tell her to radio for help and then bring her back here.'

James thought for a moment. 'You might get lost.'

Mandy hesitated. 'We're not very far from the yak trail. If you keep on whistling, I'll know where you are, and I'll whistle back, so you'll be able to find me again.'

'OK. I'll whistle three times when I'm on my way back with Mei Ling.'

'Remember, try not to make too much noise. The mother panda's somewhere close and we don't want to make things worse by startling her!'

When James was gone, Mandy waited for the stillness of the forest to descend again. Although they'd both tried hard not to, she knew that she and James had made a lot of noise as they had traversed the thick foliage and undergrowth.

When James whistled once, she whistled in reply, and then, very slowly, she started to follow the trail of the crushed grass that the injured panda had left in her wake. Periodically, Mandy checked the ground for signs of blood. After that horrible first dark pool, she found another, and then another. Her stomach tight, Mandy went on; the going was easier in the path cleared by the giant panda. She had travelled maybe fifty metres by the time she heard James whistle three times to let her know that he had found Mei Ling.

Mandy whistled her reply and then continued cautiously. She sensed that the mother panda was very near. Then she saw a pile of panda droppings, and at last, behind a bamboo plant, a glimpse of oily black fur.

Mandy stopped in her tracks. For a minute, she did not breathe. Then she reached out and, very gently, parted the bamboo leaves so that she could have a better look.

The panda was slumped listlessly on the ground. Mandy stood up on tiptoe and peered over. She could see that the paw of one of the panda's rear legs was swollen to almost twice the size of the other one. Her heart turned over. Terrified that the animal was dead, she kept watching it until she saw the rise of her chest as the panda inhaled.

Dizzy with relief, Mandy stepped back. James's whistle came from nearby. She'd been concentrating so hard on the panda that she hadn't heard his last few calls. She whistled once and then carefully made her way back to the place where they had found the deer trap.

Mei Ling was white with shock. 'I've called for help,' her voice trembled. 'The workers should be with us in ten minutes or so. Mandy, your parents are coming with my mother from the research station. They will come as soon as they can. I'll go back to the yak trail so I can show them the way.'

As they watched Mei Ling go, James turned to Mandy. 'What can we do now?' James asked.

'All we can do is wait,' Mandy replied, as she gazed at her watch and willed the time to pass.

Although it seemed like an age, within ten minutes Mandy heard a slight rustle of branches. She looked up to see Rick making his way swiftly through the forest. He held up his hand to let her know that he had seen her.

'Where is the panda?' he asked in a tense whisper.

'About fifty metres away, behind that bamboo bush,' Mandy told him, pointing in the direction of the bush.

'Has she moved?'

'Not since I've been here.'

Moving slowly, Rick made his way towards the bush. Once he'd seen the panda he stood watching for a moment and then he moved back and began to walk in a wide circle around her. Mandy and James followed his progress by watching for flashes of the colourful mountaineering jacket that he wore.

When Rick had completed his circuit, he walked farther away and then he spoke into his radio receiver. When the crackling reply came, he spoke again.

'What he's doing?' James asked.

Mandy was watching intently. 'I'm not sure,' she whispered. 'I think he's organising people to surround the panda in case she moves. I know they're waiting for Mum to come with her treatment kit.'

At that moment, Mei Ling appeared with two of the research station workers. While Rick was telling them what to do, Mei Ling joined Mandy and James. 'Mrs Hope will be here soon,' she said.

Mandy's heart was in her mouth. The panda seemed very ill to her. She was afraid that its life would ebb away before help arrived. 'What about the cub?' she asked Mei Ling.

Rick looked over at them anxiously. 'Stop talking!' he mouthed. Mei Ling looked at Mandy; they both felt so helpless. Now that they were standing still, the bitter winter air felt colder than ever. Mandy glanced at her watch and saw that it was the afternoon now. The time had flown past.

She glanced up at the sky, which was already darkening in the east. A large single snowflake fell and landed on her nose where it melted. She shivered, knowing that, when night came, the bitter chill would not help the injured panda.

When Rick finished making his radio calls he beckoned them over. 'This is the plan of action,' he said, softly. 'We're now in place around the panda. When Emily arrives, we'll close in a little, taking care not to startle her. As soon as Emily's in place with the dart gun, we'll let her know that we're here.'

Mei Ling nodded. 'How badly has the panda been hurt?' she asked him.

'I'm not a vet,' Rick replied, 'but I guess she's got an infection like Li Li. She's obviously had the cut a while, and it looks much deeper than the one Li Li had. Because it's her rear paw, she can't move easily and if she panics and tries to get up she might cause herself further damage.'

His explanation was interrupted by a radio call. Mandy heard her mother's voice asking if he could estimate how large the panda was. 'I'd say eighty kilos or less,' Rick replied.

Mandy turned to Mei Ling. 'My mother's working out the dose of antibiotics that she will need to use,' she explained in a whisper.

'How big is the cut?' Emily Hope's voice asked.

'It extends right into the pad of one toe and through the fur above,' Rick replied. 'The next toe is torn too, but not as badly.'

'It sounds as if it will need anaesthesia. I think I know all I need to know. Thanks for your help,' Mrs Hope said briskly.

'You're welcome,' Rick replied. Mandy remembered how her mother and father had helped to anaesthetise an elephant in Africa, but then there had been an experienced local vet to help. Now the Hopes were on their own.

'Is anyone coming from Wolong?' she asked Rick anxiously.

He shook his head. 'The roads are virtually impassable. They may get through later this evening, but we haven't time to wait for them.'

Mandy and James looked at each other. 'Don't worry,' James said, 'I'm sure your mum and dad will manage.'

'Mrs Hope treated Li Li successfully,' Mei Ling added.

Mandy said nothing. The injury sounded much more serious than Li Li's had been and, although she knew that her parents were excellent vets, she was worried that the panda might be beyond help.

* * *

Adam Hope arrived first with a heavy bag of equipment, closely followed by Emily Hope who carried another. Dr Yun and one of her assistants carried a large chest between them and a second assistant brought a portable light and a battery pack.

'What are you going to do, Mum?' Mandy asked.

Emily Hope's face was serious. 'First of all I'm going to try to have a look at her,' she said, as Rick led her through the undergrowth. Mandy's eyes followed as her mum and dad walked closer to the panda.

The Hopes returned a minute later. 'She has to be anaesthetised,' Emily said firmly, as Adam nodded in agreement. Mrs Hope took a vial from her bag and loaded the contents into a dart gun after looking up the correct dosage from a chart. Rick made a radio call to the vet at Wolong and then handed the receiver to her.

Mandy listened as her mother went through the process of putting a wild giant panda under a general anaesthetic. 'It's not something that's been done many times before,' her dad remarked grimly.

'In fact, only once that I know of,' Rick agreed.

Tension gripped Mandy; she knew that

anaesthetising any animal carried a small risk that was multiplied many times when the procedure was carried out in the wild.

Emily checked the dart gun and then loaded another one, which she handed to Adam.

Adam Hope put his hand on her shoulder. 'Don't worry, you treated Li Li successfully, and we can call Wolong or even Chengdu Zoo if you need some help.'

Emily Hope took off her woolly hat and tied her hair back carefully, before putting on a surgical cap. Adam tied a gown over her clothes and then she put on two pairs of rubber gloves.

'Can we watch?' Mandy pleaded.

Emily and Adam glanced at each other, then at Rick, who nodded. 'I think you deserve to,' he said, 'so long as you promise not to get in the way.'

'We won't!' Mandy and James said together.

'I won't, either,' Mei Ling added.

Mrs Hope gathered up the equipment she needed and then turned to them. 'Right, I'm ready,' she said, determinedly. 'At least, I'm as ready as I'll ever be.'

Rick lead them through the forest – Emily followed by Adam, Dr Yun and her assistants, with Mandy, James and Mei Ling bringing up the rear. As they approached the panda, Rick stood aside and said to the two vets, 'It's best if you let her see you first. That way she'll be less traumatised than if you simply dart her from behind.'

Emily nodded. 'I'll have to aim for a large muscle,' she said. 'I'll start with a low dose and then we can increase it if need be.'

Emily and Adam Hope walked forward and Mandy, James and Mei Ling waited behind Rick. The panda seemed to be asleep, but she appeared to sense the approach of humans and opened one eye warily.

The giant panda gazed at the vets for a minute

before she dropped her head down between her front legs, hiding her eyes with her paws.

'Why is she doing that?' James asked Mei Ling.

'It's what pandas do when they are afraid,' she replied.

'She's too sick and tired to do anything else,' Rick added.

Emily Hope stood very still for a moment, and then, when the panda seemed settled, she lifted the dart gun and aimed. With a soft pop, the dart of anaesthetic hit the panda's shoulder.

The panda jerked in surprise but then, as the drug quickly took effect, she slumped to one side. Mandy sighed with relief when she saw that the panda hadn't fallen on her injured paw and they wouldn't have to move her.

'Well done!' James congratulated Emily Hope.

Once the panda was completely asleep, the two vets approached and began to examine her gently. Mandy watched with bated breath. She glanced at Mei Ling, who was biting her lip, and Dr Yun, who was watching intently.

Once the Hopes had completed their examination, they came over to let the others know the result.

'One toe's damaged beyond repair,' Emily explained. 'There's evidence of infection too so

I'll have to amputate the damaged portion. The other one can be cleaned and stitched.'

'Will she still be able to walk?' Mandy asked anxiously.

'I think so,' Emily replied. 'I'm just going to call the vets at Wolong and go through the procedure with them.'

Everyone waited anxiously as Emily talked to an expert panda vet. The conversation went on for quite a while; Emily's only response was to occasionally murmur in agreement and scribble down some notes.

Once the call was over, she asked Adam to help sort out the right equipment as Dr Yun's assistant set up the light.

'I'm going to have to operate here,' Emily said, as she put on a fresh pair of surgical gloves. 'The injury's too serious for us to try to move her.'

Rick nodded. 'And it will save valuable time.'

'Can you organise help to set up a treatment area?' Emily asked.

'Sure.' Rick went off to speak to the workers.

'Will the panda be OK?' Mandy asked.

Her mother smiled tiredly. 'I hope so. I'm going to sew up the wound with soluble stitches so that there's no need to remove them. Then I'll put on a dissolving anti-bacterial dressing as well, which along with antibiotics should deal with the infection. She'll be pretty dopey for a day or two because of the anaesthetic, but afterwards she should make a good recovery. If she has problems, we can always move her then. But what I'd like to do is to see her stay in the wild.'

Mandy and James exchanged a meaningful glance.

'I think it's best if you go back to the research station,' Emily Hope said, as she checked the time. 'The operation is going to take quite a while and it's time you two and Mei Ling had something to eat.'

'And then you should get some sleep,' Adam added firmly, 'since you were up most of last night.'

Dr Yun saw the disappointment that spread over their faces. 'Don't worry,' she said kindly, 'the panda will still be here tomorrow. You'll all be able to come back to see her then.'

'Why don't you come with me to see how the cub's doing?' Rick offered. He had finished explaining to the workers what they needed to do and had come over to join them.

'You're not staying?' Mandy asked, astonished.

The big Canadian shook his head. 'I'm not a vet and, besides, someone should keep an eye on the cub.'

Eight

In the pen Rick had built behind the research station, he had erected a tent made from pine branches and a tarpaulin. The little panda cub was lying under it, sleeping peacefully on a pile of sterile robes. The cub's forepaws covered his eyes, and his black-and-white body was curled into a tight ball.

Mandy noticed that, beside him, a variety of food had been left: tender young bamboo shoots and leaves and a pile of vegetables. The food looked untouched to her.

Rick saw her concern. 'I don't want the little guy to get too hungry,' he said. 'So I decided to try some treats to tempt him to eat.'

Mandy nodded. 'He seems content enough.'

Rick frowned. 'He was crying earlier. He misses his mother terribly. I guess the little guy just tired himself out. Once Emily's finished his mother's treatment, I'm thinking of taking some of the scrubs she's used to let him smell his mother again. That might give him some hope.'

'Has he eaten anything?' James asked.

'It doesn't look like it. But he's plump enough. He should be fine for another day or two.'

Mandy flinched. 'Surely his mother will be better before that!'

Rick shrugged. 'It can take a wild animal a long time to recover from a general anaesthetic. It might be twenty-four hours or more before she knows him again.'

Mei Ling smiled weakly. She had been listening patiently to Mandy and James's questions. 'Come on,' she suggested, 'let's go and see what's for dinner.'

They left the Canadian with the cub and approached the hut. Tantalising smells greeted them as they opened the door. The meal the cook had prepared was delicious, but as Mandy began to eat, tiredness overwhelmed her. The cook saw her drooping eyelids and packed her off to bed, along with James and Mei Ling.

As she fell into an exhausted sleep, Mandy gave a last thought to the mother panda, hoping fervently that she had survived her treatment and would soon be reunited with her cub.

In the morning, Mandy raised the blind to see the sun shining through a break in the clouds. In the next cubicle, James was still asleep. After Mandy had dressed she woke James, then hurried ahead to the common room, where her father and Mei Ling were finishing breakfast.

Adam Hope held his hand up as if to field Mandy's first question of the day. 'The mother panda's fine,' he said. 'The cut was even deeper than it seemed at first, but we radioed the vet at Wolong and your mother managed to treat it successfully. The panda still hasn't come out of the anaesthetic, but Dr Yun and Rick are watching over her. I'm going to join them just as soon as I've had something to eat.'

'Where's Mum?'

Adam yawned. 'Sleeping, Mandy. That's what normal people do when they get tired.'

Mandy grinned at her father's familiar teasing and sat down to a breakfast of rolls and tea. She'd had little to eat yesterday and ate ravenously now.

James joined her sleepily just as she'd finished her third roll.

'Hey, leave some for me!' James said, eyeing the diminishing plate of food. He pulled up a chair. 'How's the panda?'

James let out a huge sigh of relief when Mandy told him that the cub's mother was doing well. As James helped himself to the rolls and hot tea, Adam Hope stood up. 'I'm going to see the panda,' he said.

'Wait for us!' Mandy cried.

Adam Hope shook his head. 'It's just a check-up. You can come along later,' he said. 'She'll be sleeping most of the day, I promise you. You're not going to miss anything by finishing your breakfast.'

Mandy's instinct told her that her father was hiding something from her, but he had gone before she had a chance to ask him what. She and James helped Mei Ling to clear the dishes and wash up and then they went to see the cub. On the way Mei Ling went into the research station to talk to her mother on the radio. When she emerged, there was a frown on her face.

'What's the matter?' Mandy asked her.

'The panda's injury was very severe; she may not make a full recovery,' Mei Ling told her. 'Mrs Hope is not sure if she can stay in the wild or not. Last night they wanted to take her and her cub to Wolong, but because of the storm they could not.'

James looked at the sky. 'The weather's fine now.'

'Yes,' Mei Ling replied, 'but there was a bad storm at Wolong yesterday. The weather report says it will come here today.'

Mandy's stomach tightened with fear. 'But Dad said the mother panda was doing well.'

'She is,' Mei Ling agreed, 'but they do not know what she'll be like when she recovers from the anaesthetic. Only one panda has had such a bad injury before. That panda was taken to Wolong for treatment and although he recovered he could not return to the wild. He's still at the Wolong Centre. Mr Hope told me that Mrs Hope does not know what the panda's chances are until the animal fully wakes up. It's possible that she will be sleepy for several days.'

Mandy swallowed nervously.

'But she'll be able to take care of her cub, won't she?' James queried.

Mei Ling shrugged. 'We don't know.'

The panda cub was still curled up in a ball, but he was awake. Mandy gazed at him from the safety of a bamboo fence that ringed the compound where he was kept. The panda stared back at her through his slitted pupils; Mandy knew that pandas' eyesight was poor, but that he would know she was there because of his excellent sense of smell.

After a moment, the cub turned away as if in disgust.

'He's missing his mother,' James explained, seeing the hurt expression on Mandy's face.

Mandy nodded. 'I know, I just so want to help him.'

Mei Ling had been to the kitchen, and come back with some choice bits of steamed vegetables piled on the end of a long spade. Very slowly, she lifted it over the fence and then tipped the vegetables on to a bamboo leaf in front of the cub.

Mandy held her breath as the cub approached the vegetables, then she sighed in despair as he turned away. The cub constantly sniffed the air in what they assumed was a forlorn attempt to find his mother.

'Hello, little one,' Mandy whispered, when the panda cub's gaze passed over her again. 'I'm Mandy, and this is James and Mei Ling. We're your friends and we're going to look after you. We're going to take you back to your mother soon.'

The panda began to wail, a pitiful mewling at first and then a high-pitched howl that filled the yard and echoed faintly in the still mountain air.

Mandy's stomach tightened in sympathy; she could not bear to see any animal in distress.

She turned to Mei Ling. 'What can we do?' she asked desperately.

Mei Ling's eyes glistened with tears. 'There's nothing we can do, Mandy,' she said. 'When Rick comes back, he is going to bring something that smells of the cub's mother. Maybe that will comfort him a little.'

James looked at Mandy. 'Let's go and see if we can help,' he said.

They reached the place where the mother panda was still sleeping and collapsed out of breath. They had run all the way there. The panda was curled up under a tarpaulin held up with posts which provided a little shelter against the wind and the snow. Mandy, James and Mei Ling quickly spoke to Dr Yun, who left immediately to see if she could persuade the cub to eat.

'The cub's terribly upset,' Mandy told Rick. 'We need to take something to him quickly.'

Rick scratched his beard thoughtfully. 'We were just talking about that. I'm not sure that it is a good idea after all to give the cub the scrubs to smell.'

'Pandas use their sense of smell like we use hearing,' Adam Hope explained. 'The trouble is, if the cub gets a whiff of his mother's blood, he might think she's dead. And also, we know that pandas communicate with each other through smell and it might be that the mother has released some sort of scent that would tell the cub that she was badly hurt.'

Mei Ling nodded knowingly. James scratched his head. 'Are there any other ways pandas communicate with one another?' he asked.

A smile spread over Rick's worried face. 'Yes, they have a sort of bulletin board arrangement,' he explained. 'In the wild, you find certain trees where a number of pandas will leave their scent in the form of urine. We think they leave messages for one another.'

'What about hearing?'

'We're not sure about that. A mother hears her cub's cries, we think – panda cubs cry just as much as human babies – but whether adult pandas communicate with one another by sound is another matter.'

James nodded thoughtfully. 'What were you thinking?' Mandy asked him.

Her friend wrinkled his nose. 'Your dad's got his video camera with him. I was just wondering if we could tape the noise of the mother's breathing and play it to the cub, or maybe tape his cries to get her to wake up.'

Adam Hope shook his head vigorously. 'We've got to let her wake up naturally. Unfortunately that may take the best part of the day. Anyway, I don't think the microphone is sensitive enough to pick up the sound of breathing.' He glanced up at the sky. 'Certainly not with the way the wind is picking up.'

Mandy shivered as she listened to the icy gale. 'I don't suppose there is any point in picking up some of the grass and bamboo leaves near where she was found, is there? Or do you think the cub might sense her fear from that as well?'

Rick did not reply as he thought about it. Mandy heard the rustle of leaves and looked around to see her mother arriving. Emily Hope gave her a quick hug before going to examine her patient. First of all she listened carefully to the panda's chest.

'There's no sign of the infection spreading to her lungs,' she said. 'So that's good. But she's still unconscious. I don't have any idea when she's going to come round.'

'She will wake up, won't she?' Mandy asked anxiously.

'Of course she will,' Emily reassured her. 'It's just a question of how she reacts to the fact that she's lost a bit of her foot. She'll still be able to walk on it, but she won't be quite as sure-footed as she was before. At least, not at first.'

'We might be lucky,' Adam Hope remarked. 'After all, the same thing happens to dogs and cats all the time and they're usually happy enough. A bear can survive an injury to its foot.'

'Hmm, I wonder,' Emily said, thoughtfully. 'The truth is that we don't really know, and we certainly won't find out until she wakes up.'

Rick rubbed his beard. 'Your idea about the grass, Mandy,' he announced, 'it's worth a try. It's certainly better than doing nothing.'

They set off through the forest to the place where James had found the deer trap. The mark left by the panda's body was still clearly visible in the frosted grass. Rick considered it for a while and then began to search around.

'What are you doing?' James asked.

'Trying to see if there might be one of these panda bulletin boards anywhere around,' Rick explained. 'It's not likely this far down the mountain, but it's always possible. It's usually a tree stump or something like that. Usually you can clearly see scratch marks that the pandas also leave.'

'And if we find one?' Mandy said.

'I'll shave some of the bark off and let the cub smell that, because I'm sure there wouldn't be the aura of pain and fear that there might be from the grass.'

'We should give it a go,' James suggested, practically. Rick handed out gloves and gowns and they all began to gather grass and leaves and fragments of bark that they found nearby. When their arms were full, they headed up to the research station.

Mei Ling's teeth were chattering. 'My hands are very cold,' she complained. 'I can't feel my fingers!'

Mandy was glad she'd brought along the waterproof gloves that her grandparents had given her for Christmas. Her hands were comfortably warm. She stopped and put down her carefully wrapped bundle of grass, then took off the gloves and handed them to Mei Ling, who put them on gratefully.

As he approached the panda cub, Rick walked very slowly. The little animal was still curled up defensively and Mandy could tell from the slight movement in the cub's body that he was alert and ready to move quickly if necessary. Rick studied the cub for a moment and then he turned to the others.

'I'm not sure how to do this,' Rick said, pensively. Mei Ling pointed to the spade, but he shook his head.

'How about if you put the bundles just inside the fence,' James suggested. 'If you pull the wraps away, the cub shouldn't smell us on them. If he smells fear, then he can keep away from it, but if he smells something comforting, then he can amble over.'

'Sounds like a good idea,' Mandy said.

'Yeah,' Rick agreed. 'Why not?'

Mandy, James and Mei Ling watched nervously as Rick hefted the bundles over the fence and then whipped the wraps away. The cub did not move as he gazed at Rick.

A moment later, Mandy noticed that the cub's nose was twitching. She watched intently as he sniffed again and then began to make his way over towards the grass. Rick peered at the little panda thoughtfully. 'I should have gotten the camera and recorded this.'

'I'll get Dad's, if you like,' Mandy offered.

Before the Canadian had a chance to reply, Mei Ling's radio chirruped into life. She pressed Receive and then held it to her ear.

Everybody heard Emily's voice announce that the mother panda was showing signs that she was coming round from the anaesthetic. Mandy could detect the tension in her mother's normally calm voice.

'We'd better get the cub back to her quickly!' James cried.

Rick shook his head. 'There's no hurry. It's more important to return him safely, without her knowing that we've been carrying him. If she's anything like the pandas I've seen anaesthetised in zoos, it'll be some time before she wakes up properly.'

Nine

As dark storm clouds gathered in the sky above, Rick made a pile of everything he would need to carry the panda cub back to his mother and then Mei Ling tied a surgical gown over his clothes. Once Rick had surgical gloves on, he stepped over the fence and into the compound, where the tiny cub gazed at him for a moment before it stood up slowly. The cub let Rick approach to within a metre of him, and then he jumped up playfully and ran nimbly over to the other corner of the compound.

Rick froze. The cub almost seemed to be grinning. 'He's having fun!' Mandy whispered in amazement.

Rick turned around, holding a finger to his lips. Then he gestured for Mandy, Mei Ling and James each to take up a position at the other three corners of the pen. Mei Ling frowned, and indicated frantically to Rick that they needed more people to guard the edges. Rick shook his head. 'He's not big enough to climb over,' he mouthed.

'I don't think we should take the risk,' Mei Ling argued.

Rick nodded in agreement and Mei Ling hurried off to the research station, coming out with the radio operator before she fetched two assistants who were sleeping in the accommodation hut, along with the cook, who came out rubbing her floury hands on her apron. She was complaining vigorously in Chinese.

'She doesn't like being disturbed when she's making noodles,' Mei Ling smiled.

Rick watched anxiously until all four were in position, along with Mandy, James and Mei Ling at the corners. In his corner, the panda cub gazed at the humans, and then dropped his head between his front legs, covering his eyes.

Mandy held her breath. Rick held up an arm to tell everyone to keep completely still. He then waited for several minutes. When the panda cub's posture didn't change, he walked slowly but purposefully towards him. The cub jumped and Rick frantically signalled to Mei Ling to guard her corner carefully. The cub looked round and then suddenly zoomed right across the pen and somersaulted over the bamboo fence in the narrow gap between Mandy and the cook, who shrieked in surprise.

The cub landed on his back at Mandy's feet. She had to hug herself to stifle her impulse to pick him up, for fear of transferring her smell to the cub.

Rick jumped the fence and came round behind Mandy. The cub took one look at him and then fled towards the pine trees.

'I was afraid this would happen,' Rick grunted as he set off after it, with Mandy and the others following. The panda cub paused at the first conifer and then began to thrash through the undergrowth.

Mei Ling tugged frantically at Mandy's arm. 'Don't chase him.' She shook her head, as Rick stopped at the place where the cub had disappeared. 'We'll have to go into the forest beyond the cub and then cut him off. If we let him go deeper, he'll get lost again.'

Mandy nodded. 'That makes sense.'

Rick motioned frantically for silence as he

walked over to them. 'The cub's just underneath the first pine tree,' he whispered. 'We'll have to corner him. I'll go and get some more help.'

They all waited anxiously until Rick returned with as many workers as he could find. 'Mandy, James and Mei Ling, you go into the trees on either side of the cub,' he began. 'When you're twenty paces inside the forest, stop. I'll whistle when we're all in position. Then walk slowly to the cub. When I whistle twice, start running. The cub will run away and I'll catch him.'

Her heart thudding, Mandy walked along the edge of the pine trees and then began to clamber through the thick foliage of conifer and bamboo. The undergrowth was so dense that inside the forest it was dark and difficult to see far ahead. Mandy counted her steps carefully and then waited to hear Rick's whistle.

She remembered sadly the stories she'd heard of pandas who become too accustomed to humans ever to be returned to the wild. Her instinct was to try to comfort the little cub but she knew that was not the right thing to do if he was to have a chance of returning to his mother and his life in the wild.

When Rick whistled, Mandy began to move very slowly in the direction of the cub. All around, she heard the rustle of leaves as the others did the same thing. She had to stop herself laughing at the chatter of angry Chinese as the cook struggled through the thick vegetation; Mandy imagined she was muttering about the green streaks on her apron.

Mandy's attention was quickly drawn back to the little cub that they were in fear of losing again. All she could see around her was the deep green of the forest and she could not work out exactly where she was. She became anxious until she spotted the dull mud of the compound through some pine branches a few metres away.

Once she had got her bearings back, Mandy walked forward another two steps. Suddenly she caught sight of a glimpse of white fur. The panda cub was crouched under the pine tree, precisely where Rick said he would be. Mandy could see only his back, but she could tell that he was poised to flee.

She stayed very still until she heard Rick's double whistle and then she rushed forward. The cub turned his head in alarm and then dashed out from his hiding-place.

Mandy emerged from the forest to see the little cub streaking over the compound with Rick in hot pursuit. Her heart was hammering as she watched. The panda cub was surprisingly quick and even more nimble than Rick.

He was still trying to play a game with Rick, pausing every so often to let him catch up.

As soon as Rick realised what the cub was doing, he stood very still in his gown, holding a length of surgical sheet like a bullfighter. As the cub dived this way and that, the Canadian remained motionless. Mandy held her breath as the cub paused and sat back. He looked sad because the game was over. Then a glint appeared in the cub's slitted eyes and he dashed off in the direction of the kitchen.

With speed that was amazing considering his size, Rick managed to catch the cub with a

combination of a rugby tackle and using the sheet as a lasso. The cub cried with indignation as Mandy breathed a huge sigh of relief.

'At last!' James gasped besides her. For the first time that morning, Mei Ling's tense frown gave way to a grin.

Rick McGinley led the procession, with Mandy, James and Mei Ling following. In his swaddling of green surgical sheets the cub mewled in protest, but he seemed to have abandoned the idea of escape. The big Canadian ambled along slowly, his wide face a picture of concern as he concentrated on carrying the cub safely back to his mother.

'Rick could almost be his father!' James joked.

Mandy giggled. 'You're right,' she agreed.

Mei Ling grinned. 'The workers call Rick *Daxiongmao*, that's Chinese for panda.'

Mandy and James laughed. Rick certainly seemed happiest when he was working with the pandas.

Dr Yun met them at the yak trail. 'The mother's still sleeping,' she said, 'but she could wake up at any time.'

'Good,' Rick said, as he continued to make his way through the forest to the clearing where the giant panda lay. Emily and Adam Hope were watching over her anxiously. The panda's injured rear leg had been wrapped in a stretchy bandage.

'Will you have to take the bandage off?' Mandy asked her mother.

'Well, she's going to be pretty dopey for a day or two with the effects of the anaesthetic and the antibiotics, so she won't be moving around much, but it is quite possible that the bandage will come off by itself – we'll just have to wait and see. The main thing is to keep the wound clean and dry until initial healing takes place,' Emily explained.

'The workers will keep a very close watch on her for the next few days,' Dr Yun added. 'They'll make sure she has plenty of bamboo leaves and shoots, and that she doesn't hurt herself.'

Adam Hope folded his arms. 'We hope she will be able to recover here, Mandy. If she doesn't she'll have to be taken to Wolong, and their experience is that once a panda's taken into captivity for treatment, it will never return to the wild.'

'But aren't all the pandas going to Wolong?' James queried.

'That's the plan,' Dr Yun confirmed. 'But they won't be taken into captivity. The Wolong Centre is the biggest panda reserve in China – it's just like the wild but it's a protected environment – like a wildlife park. Our pandas will be safe there, and they'll be able to mingle with others.'

Rick signalled that he was ready to let the cub go. Nobody spoke as the big Canadian kneeled down and deposited the bundle on the ground. The cub's head popped up in surprise, then he sniffed expectantly. As he sat up, Rick deftly pulled away the sheet in which he had carried the cub.

The cub sniffed furiously in his mother's direction and then scampered to her. When he was within centimetres of her, he stopped and wailed. The mother panda shifted her position slightly, but she didn't open her eyes.

The cub crawled around his sleeping mother, pausing at her heavily bandaged rear foot. He plonked down and gently stroked it, crying to himself. Then he crept up to her stomach, where he eased himself between her forelegs and snuggled close to her.

An audible sigh came from the people gathered around. Mandy brushed a tear from her eye. Even James, standing next to her, blinked.

The cub was silent for a moment, and then he began to whimper.

Dr Yun and Rick were watching intently, as were the Hopes. Emily's mouth formed a thin line and Adam looked tired and stressed.

'At least the cub is safely back with her, but we'll

have to wait to see what happens when she wakes up,' Emily said to Mandy, just as the first huge snowflakes began to drop from the sullen winter sky.

For some time, the panda mother didn't move, then slowly she turned over, nearly squashing the cub, who emerged from underneath her with a pitiful wail. The mother panda opened her eyes for a moment, then closed them again.

Mandy gasped.

With his tail between his legs, the little cub crawled round his mother's huge body and snuggled into her again.

Dr Yun was shaking her head. 'We'll have to watch them both carefully until she's properly awake,' she said. 'As you can see, sometimes when panda mothers are sleeping they roll over and smother their cubs. Even when she wakes up this mother is bound to be dopey from the anaesthetic so we'll have to keep an eye on her.'

Mandy frowned. 'That must be an awful thing for a panda mother to discover she's done,' she whispered.

'It is,' Dr Yun agreed. 'They go into a profound depression. It's very sad to watch.'

Snow was falling heavily now and settling on the branches of trees. One of the workers from the research station lit the battery light, which made a small yellow pool on the dark forest floor.

In her thick jacket, Mandy shivered.

'The little guy certainly knows that he's found his mom,' Rick pointed out. 'That's a good sign.'

Dr Yun nodded her agreement.

'It's just a question of waiting until she wakes up,' Emily said. 'He's had plenty of time around her, so she should be able to smell herself on him. But we've absolutely no idea of how she's going to react when she comes around.'

Adam Hope rubbed his chin thoughtfully. 'We do know that other mammals have managed well enough. Farm animals are always OK and so are big cats, I believe.'

'But pandas are unique in several respects,' Emily countered. 'They don't respond to help from humans in the way some other animals do. They are proud and independent creatures.'

Just then, a chunk of snow fell from a branch of pine, landing besides the pandas with a plop. Mandy shivered.

'There's still a chance that she's going to reject her cub,' Rick said soberly.

Ten

Mandy's nose and cheeks shone bright red from the icy wind and snow. They had been standing watching the panda and her cub for nearly an hour and it was difficult to ignore the cold weather that had closed in on them. The mother panda was still sleeping despite the cub beside her whimpering plaintively. Mandy glanced at her watch and hoped fervently that the mother would wake soon. She couldn't bear another night of not knowing what the fate of the mother and cub would be.

Beside Mandy, James shifted nervously. They were standing in a wide circle round the pandas, all eyes fixed in the same direction, watching eagerly for any sign of the mother panda waking.

Several times, Emily Hope had crept closer to the panda to listen to her breathing, which had remained stable.

Mandy's dad came over to where Mandy was standing and put his arm round her. 'Don't worry,' he reassured her, 'sleep is nature's way of healing.'

Emily brushed away a stray strand of hair that had fallen over her face. 'It's a pity nature can't heal a septic foot too!' she joked, tiredly.

Mandy was afraid that it was going to be a long wait.

A short distance from the clearing the pandas were in, Mei Ling had set up a portable gas stove, where she was making tea. Mandy could smell the aroma of the tea leaves as well as something more substantial. She turned and saw the beaming cook with a huge tray of spring rolls, followed by two workers who were struggling with a vast tin pot full of noodles. When a makeshift table had been set up everyone fell on the food ravenously, including Mandy and James.

The cook grinned delightedly as the hungry panda-watchers devoured the meal. Her cheerful chatter told Mandy that she had recovered from her ordeal that morning with the panda cub and she was wearing a clean apron free from grass stains.

Mandy felt better when she had eaten, although as soon as she returned to watch the pandas, the cub's mewling began to worry her again.

'Try not to think about it,' James suggested.

'I can't help it,' she replied. 'The poor cub must be starving, he hasn't eaten for nearly two days. I feel guilty because my stomach's full.'

Mandy sensed a movement behind her and as she turned was taken aback to see Tai An, who glanced briefly at her before he walked over to talk to Dr Yun.

Mandy gasped, wondering what the Chinese boy was doing here. She held her hand over her mouth hoping Tai An would understand it as a sign that she had kept his secret, but he didn't look in her direction.

'What are they talking about?' James asked Mei Ling in a whisper.

Mei Ling shook her head. 'I can't hear.'

Mandy gazed at the zoologist and the young boy. They were just out of earshot of the others and they had been talking for a while. Tai An was gesticulating with his arms as Dr Yun listened expressionlessly. 'From his body language, it looks like he's trying to explain something.'

James's eyes widened. 'You don't think he's lost another trap?'

Mandy gulped. 'Surely not!'

'Don't worry,' Mei Ling told them, 'the workers have been busy searching for traps with a metal detector. They have found half a dozen – many more than could have belonged to Tai An. They do not blame him for what happened.'

Mandy nodded sympathetically. Tai An finished his part of the conversation and Dr Yun began to reply to him. She seemed to be explaining something to Tai An.

The boy listened intently for a while, and then, all of a sudden, his posture changed. He stood proudly upright and then dipped his head in the Chinese gesture that shows gratitude. Dr Yun smiled broadly and then patted his shoulder before she called to the cook to bring him some food.

Tai An ate hungrily, but Mandy noticed that he took only the noodles that were served to him. He put the spring rolls in the cotton shoulder bag that he carried, obviously to take back to his family. Once he finished eating, he came over to talk to them.

Mandy went to meet him. 'I kept my promise,' she told him. 'Nobody knows that you helped.'

Tai An smiled shyly. 'I thought about it all last

night,' he said. 'This morning, I talked to my mother and grandfather. We agreed that I should confess to Dr Yun that I set the trap. That way, if the panda injury is reported, at least I can prove that I told the truth.'

Mandy nodded as they joined James and Mei Ling.

Tai An's expression remained sad. 'I'm very angry with myself for setting the trap that hurt the panda,' he announced. 'Big mistake. Not only did I hurt the panda, I am afraid that I will bring bad luck on my family.'

'No!' James cried. 'It was you who saved the panda, Tai An. Without you, we would never have found the mother.'

'And the cub would have been doomed to live in captivity at best,' Mandy added. 'Now they've both got a chance of staying in the wild.'

Tai An's gloom lifted a little. 'That's what Dr Yun told me,' he said. 'She has offered me a job finding deer traps. It will mean because of the money I'll earn I won't have to trap deer myself any more.'

'That's excellent!' Mandy exclaimed.

Tai An looked doubtful. 'The mother panda is not awake yet. There is still a chance she will be taken into captivity,' he said. Mei Ling replied with a burst of Chinese, which Tai An answered equally vigorously.

When she noticed Mandy and James's confusion, Mei Ling grinned. 'Sorry. We are debating the captive-breeding programme. I argue it is better than nothing. Tai An says that the Chinese people should be ashamed about the plight of the giant panda. It's our fault that the species is in danger.'

'It's not your fault, personally, Tai An,' Mandy pointed out. 'You're doing all you can to save the panda. It's not the only animal that's been driven to near-extinction by humans.'

'And don't forget the panda's greed for bamboo leaves!' James added. 'Giant pandas can eat anything, but they insist on feeding on bamboo. If they were a bit more adventurous in their eating habits, then there would be enough food for all of them.'

Everyone laughed, including Rick, who had come over to listen.

'The same thing has happened to wild animals all over the world,' he told them. 'In my country, Canada, people hunted whales until very recently and several species of whales are in a similar plight to the panda. In America the manatee, one of the gentlest aquatic mammals, has nearly died out because human beings kill them accidentally with their speedboats and motor cruisers.'

Tai An listened intently. 'But Western countries insist that China must save the giant pandas!' he protested.

Rick smiled. 'We're very good at telling other people what to do, but the truth is, people all over the world have made the same mistake. It makes no difference if an animal's hide is hunted for a lucky charm or a rich woman's handbag, the threat to the animals is just the same.'

Mandy nodded, agreeing wholeheartedly. Mei Ling nudged her and pointed at the sky. Night was coming, and the mother panda still hadn't properly regained consciousness yet. 'Let's go and see how the pandas are getting on,' she suggested.

Emily and Adam Hope were watching the mother and cub intently. They had moved back a few metres to give the pandas plenty of space. The cub seemed to be dozing, but every so often it gave another pathetic mewl.

'I just hope she wakes up before we're sent to bed,' James whispered in Mandy's ear. Mandy nodded vigorously; she had no intention of leaving before the mother panda had woken up.

Mandy's gaze did not leave the pandas. 'I just can't believe that we're actually in China and I'm seeing all this,' she said softly. 'It's like a dream come true.'

'I know.' James grinned as he pinched her arm playfully.

Mandy swatted his hand. 'We'll disturb the pandas!' she mouthed.

The snowfall had stopped, leaving the forest cloaked in white through which the winter moon cast puddles of weak light. The battery light had been extinguished, leaving the mother panda and her cub in shadow. As Mandy watched, she stood as still as the sleeping panda. Even her breathing was low and soft.

Each time the mother panda shifted slightly, a little gasp rose from the onlookers.

'It's extremely important not to disturb her as she comes round,' Emily Hope whispered, and Rick nodded in agreement.

'When will that be?' James asked.

Emily looked up at the sky. 'I think soon, but then I've been thinking she'll wake soon for most of today. It's like Adam says, we've just got to let nature take its course. We just have to stay until we're sure that the mother's not going to reject her cub.'

'Hmm,' Mandy frowned thoughtfully. A cloud passed over the moon, leaving the forest in darkness. Far above the trees there came the sound of the wind picking up again. Mandy huddled deeper into her jacket and tried not to shiver. She didn't want her parents to notice her discomfort because then they might decide to send her and James back to the warmth of the accommodation hut.

'Oh,' Mei Ling cried softly, as the wind blew the cloud away and the moon shone down again, leaving the mother panda and cub in a pool of faint light. Mandy and James saw that the mother's eyes had opened and she was struggling weakly to sit up against the tree trunk where she had been left.

As the mother panda hauled herself into a sitting position, the little cub slid off her chest and landed with a dull thud on the ground. He sat there for a moment, winded, and then he opened his lungs and howled.

The mother panda's nose twitched, then her dark eye patches seemed to furrow into a frown and she looked down to where the cub had fallen. She lifted a forepaw and scratched her head for a moment and then she leaned over and picked the cub up and held him tightly to her chest. She rocked him to and fro for a moment and he chortled gleefully. Then the cub began to wail again and his mother, obviously understanding his cry, very tenderly held him to her breast and stroked him softly as he began to feed.

A collective sigh rose from the group of panda-watchers. Mandy was weak with joy as Emily hugged Adam first and then her.

'Well done, Mum,' Mandy congratulated her.

Emily smiled; there were tears in her eyes. 'I'm just delighted that I managed to help.'

Mandy blinked her own tears away as James grinned broadly and Mei Ling clapped her hands in delight.

Rick pulled up the hood of his jacket. 'I guess that's it for the night. We'll leave someone on the perimeter to keep an eye on them, but I think they'll be OK together.' As he took one last look at the pandas Mandy noticed that his eyes were glistening too.

Dr Yun came over. 'I'm sure the pandas will be fine. They're clearly still bonded.'

'I'd say so,' Adam Hope nodded.

James shook his head in wonder. 'It's just as if nothing happened to her, isn't it?'

Mandy laughed as Emily Hope shot him a glance. 'I suppose that's one way of describing a major operation on a giant panda in the wild, James!'

James grinned, blushing.

'There's just one thing we have to do before we leave them,' Mei Ling said.

'What's that?' Mandy asked.

Mei Ling looked at her mother. 'We have to name them, don't we?'

Dr Yun smiled thoughtfully.

'Well, seeing as the cub likes a joke so much, what about Ha Ha?' James said, grinning.

'That sounds good to me,' Mei Ling agreed, 'but Hua Hua would be even better – it means China.'

'Perfect,' Dr Yun said, 'and what's so distinctive about the mother panda?'

'The mother was hard to track down,' Mandy began, 'and for a long time, you didn't even know she was here.'

'I know! We could call her *Bai Yu*. That means white cloud,' Dr Yun pointed out.

'That sounds just right,' Mandy said. She took a final parting look at the pandas and then turned to walk slowly back to the research station, the pain of her sprained knee apparent, now that her mind was no longer full of worry for the pandas.

Eleven

Two days later, it was time for the Hopes and James to leave the research station for the airport. They were going to spend the rest of their time at Chengdu Zoo, where they would be able to meet the zoo's pandas and Emily intended to practise her skills in acupuncture.

'It seems like we've been here for no time at all,' Mandy remarked sadly, as she finished packing her rucksack. She was leaving Mei Ling a present of a wildlife T-shirt, and Tai An the book about Indian elephants that she had read during her long flight to China.

James nodded as he wrapped his own gifts of

chocolates for Mei Ling and two new pairs of woollen socks for Tai An. 'If we'd known we were going to make new friends, we could have brought them something really good,' he said, regretfully.

'We can write to them when we get back home to Welford and send them photographs,' Mandy suggested.

That morning, they had gone to see the pandas. Bai Yu was moving round much more confidently and Hua Hua was beginning to play games with her again.

'I can't wait to get our pictures developed,' James said. They'd spent the last few days battling the weather and frantically taking photos of the pandas in the brief lulls between the storms.

Mandy nodded. 'I bet nobody in Welford will believe us when we tell them what happened.'

Adam Hope's head appeared around the curtain of Mandy's sleeping cubicle. 'Are you two ready?' he asked. 'We're due to leave just as soon as Mr Chang arrives with the Jeep.'

'Yup,' James replied.

Mandy was too busy looking gloomily out of the window. 'It's just bad luck that the weather's cleared on the day that we're due to leave,' she complained. Mr Chang was bringing another vet from the Wolong reservation to watch over Bai Yu during

the rest of her recovery, but Dr Yun and Rick were confident that she and Hua Hua would be able to survive in the wild.

'Chengdu Zoo will be interesting,' James pointed out, trying to cheer Mandy up.' And at least we're leaving knowing that the pandas here will be safe,' he said. 'Once the mating season's over, they'll start moving along the panda corridor. Rick's sure that all the pandas here will be safely in Wolong by early summer.'

'I still wish pandas could survive in the wild,' Mandy said wistfully.

'So do I, but the Wolong conservation park is

vast, and there'll be plenty of room for all of them.'

Mandy rubbed her knee thoughtfully. Although Emily Hope had treated the sprain with a bandage, the injury still ached a little and she noticed it more because she did not have the distraction of watching Bai Yu and Hua Hua. 'I just don't want to go,' she protested.

'Maybe we can come back sometime and see Hua Hua when he's grown up,' James said hopefully.

Mandy grinned at her friend. James always managed to look on the bright side. But her sadness returned as they picked up their bags to carry them to the door of the accommodation hut. Funnily enough she was going to miss the tiny cubicle and the hard, uncomfortable bed.

There was an odd silence as they reached the door that opened into the common room. Frowning, Mandy turned the handle, and then she stopped dead.

'Surprise!' Mei Ling cried, as everyone Mandy and James had met at the research station jumped out from their hiding-place in the kitchen.

Mandy blinked as she read a huge hand-written banner that said *Good-bye and good luck, Mandy and James!* Beneath the banner there were some Chinese characters and black-and-white pictures of Bai Yu and Hua Hua.

'Wow!' James exclaimed.

'The Chinese characters mean "Thank you and good luck from Bai Yu and Hua Hua",' Mei Ling translated.

Adam Hope was standing next to his wife. 'I told a little fib,' he said. 'Mr Chang isn't coming to collect us for another couple of hours, because Dr Yun, Mei Ling and Rick decided that they wanted to hold a party.'

While Mandy and James were thanking each person in turn, the grinning cook emerged from a kitchen with a tray covered in platters of their favourite Chinese foods.

'There's just one thing we need to do first,' Dr Yun told them.

'What's that?' James asked.

'Well, as you know, we're beginning the next stage of a census of all the pandas that are known to exist in the wild, so if you don't mind, we'll go over to the research station and log in to the database now. We need to add Bai Yu and Hua Hua.'

'Of course we don't mind!' Mandy said. Rick led them all across the compound; he was in a particularly good mood, laughing and cracking jokes.

'Remember what Mr Chang said about Rick

chasing the pandas along the panda corridor quick, quick, quick?' James reminded Mandy. Mandy glanced at Rick and collapsed in a fit of laughter. When she told the others what she was laughing about, they all laughed too.

'I hope it's going to turn out to be as easy as that!' Rick said jovially.

Mandy and James waited as Dr Yun logged in to the database, which was maintained at Wolong Centre.

She scrolled through the list of names until she reached the end and the computer screen showed blanks for the next additions.

'Exactly how many wild pandas are there?' Mandy asked her.

'The last intensive survey was completed a few years ago,' the zoologist replied. 'That was based on counting panda rest sites and panda droppings, and it suggested that there were then between 872 and 1352. Since then the numbers have declined a little further, although we hope that the species has stabilised now. With luck, numbers will begin to rise in the next year or so.'

'I hope so,' Mandy said passionately.

Dr Yun smiled. 'The numbers have certainly increased by two because of you and James.'

'It wasn't just us!' Mandy protested, embarrassed.

'It was Mei Ling and Tai An and my mum and dad, and you and Rick too!'

'It was certainly because of you that we were alerted to the cub, and it was also your idea to search for the other female,' Dr Yun insisted.

'You guys helped a lot,' Rick said, in his gruff, deep, Canadian accent. 'Without you, we'd never have found these pandas.'

Mandy's flushed face paled as she thought about his words.

Dr Yun logged in the details of both pandas and then, in the space marked 'researcher/finder', entered the names 'Mandy Hope & James Hunter'.

'Yes!' James cried gleefully. Mandy grinned and then blushed with embarrassment.

Once the entries were confirmed, Dr Yun logged out of the database and then closed down the computer.

'Now for the party!' Mei Ling announced, happily.

Mandy's face was wreathed in smiles as they all trooped back to the common room. 'I still can't quite believe that we helped to save both pandas,' she told Mei Ling. 'I mean, before we came here, we'd never even *seen* a panda before.'

Mei Ling put a hand on her shoulder. 'That was a good thing – nobody who knew anything about pandas would have thought to look for a panda where you insisted we searched.'

'Yeah!' Rick added gruffly. 'But I wouldn't go boasting about how much you know about pandas, if I were you.'

James' face fell. 'What would you do?'

'I'd put it down to beginner's luck,' the huge Canadian said, to laughter all around.

Mandy joined in their laughter, not caring what kind of luck had brought Bai Yu and Hua Hua to safety and enabled them to stay in the wild.

TIGER ON THE TRACK
Animal Ark in Danger, 39

Lucy Daniels

Mandy Hope's mum is spending some time abroad with a wildlife conservation organisation – and Mandy and James have been offered the chance of a lifetime: to stay with Mrs Hope during the school holidays and help protect endangered animals!

Mandy and James are visiting a tiger reserve in India, when the mother of young tigers, Bada and Chhota, goes missing. Other tigers have disappeared too, and poachers are suspected. Mandy and James are determined to help track down the real culprits. But is it too late to save the missing tigers?

GORILLA IN THE GLADE
Animal Ark in Danger, 40

Lucy Daniels

Mandy Hope's mum is spending some time abroad with a wildlife conservation organisation – and Mandy and James have been offered the chance of a lifetime: to stay with Mrs Hope during the school holidays and help protect endangered animals!

While visiting the Kahuzi National Park in Central Africa, Mandy and James help look after Jojo, an adorable baby gorilla who has been abandoned by his mother. Another female gorilla, with a newborn baby of her own, has been picked out as a potential surrogate mum. But will she be willing to take Jojo on?

ANIMAL ARK

Lucy Daniels

1	KITTENS IN THE KITCHEN	£3.99	❏
2	PONY IN THE PORCH	£3.99	❏
3	PUPPIES IN THE PANTRY	£3.99	❏
4	GOAT IN THE GARDEN	£3.99	❏
5	HEDGEHOGS IN THE HALL	£3.99	❏
6	BADGER IN THE BASEMENT	£3.99	❏
7	CUB IN THE CUPBOARD	£3.99	❏
8	PIGLET IN A PLAYPEN	£3.99	❏
9	OWL IN THE OFFICE	£3.99	❏
10	LAMB IN THE LAUNDRY	£3.99	❏
11	BUNNIES IN THE BATHROOM	£3.99	❏
12	DONKEY ON THE DOORSTEP	£3.99	❏
13	HAMSTER IN A HAMPER	£3.99	❏
14	GOOSE ON THE LOOSE	£3.99	❏
15	CALF IN THE COTTAGE	£3.99	❏
16	KOALA IN A CRISIS	£3.99	❏
17	WOMBAT IN THE WILD	£3.99	❏
18	ROO ON THE ROCK	£3.99	❏
19	SQUIRRELS IN THE SCHOOL	£3.99	❏
20	GUINEA-PIG IN THE GARAGE	£3.99	❏
21	FAWN IN THE FOREST	£3.99	❏
22	SHETLAND IN THE SHED	£3.99	❏
23	SWAN IN THE SWIM	£3.99	❏
24	LION BY THE LAKE	£3.99	❏
25	ELEPHANTS IN THE EAST	£3.99	❏
26	MONKEYS ON THE MOUNTAIN	£3.99	❏
27	DOG AT THE DOOR	£3.99	❏
28	FOALS IN THE FIELD	£3.99	❏
29	SHEEP AT THE SHOW	£3.99	❏
30	RACOONS ON THE ROOF	£3.99	❏
31	DOLPHIN IN THE DEEP	£3.99	❏
32	BEARS IN THE BARN	£3.99	❏
33	OTTER IN THE OUTHOUSE	£3.99	❏
34	WHALE IN THE WAVES	£3.99	❏
35	HOUND AT THE HOSPITAL	£3.99	❏
36	RABBITS ON THE RUN	£3.99	❏
37	HORSE IN THE HOUSE	£3.99	❏
38	PANDA IN THE PARK	£3.99	❏
	SHEEPDOG IN THE SNOW	£3.99	❏
	KITTEN IN THE COLD	£3.99	❏
	FOX IN THE FROST	£3.99	❏
	HAMSTER IN THE HOLLY	£3.99	❏
	PONIES AT THE POINT	£3.99	❏
	SEAL ON THE SHORE	£3.99	❏
	ANIMAL ARK FAVOURITES	£3.99	❏

All Hodder Children's books are available at your local bookshop, or can be ordered direct from the publisher. Just tick the titles you would like and complete the details below. Prices and availability are subject to change without prior notice.

Please enclose a cheque or postal order made payable to *Bookpoint Ltd*, and send to: Hodder Children's Books, 39 Milton Park, Abingdon, OXON OX14 4TD, UK. Email Address: orders@bookpoint.co.uk

If you would prefer to pay by credit card, our call centre team would be delighted to take your order by telephone. Our direct line *01235 400414* (lines open 9.00 am–6.00 pm Monday to Saturday, 24 hour message answering service). Alternatively you can send a fax on *01235 400454*.

TITLE		FIRST NAME		SURNAME	

ADDRESS	
DAYTIME TEL:	POST CODE

If you would prefer to pay by credit card, please complete:
Please debit my Visa/Access/Diner's Card/American Express (delete as applicable) card no:

Signature ....

Expiry Date: ....

If you would NOT like to receive further information on our products please tick the box. ❐